Chapter 1

It was a short, wet cab ride from West 76th to Penn Station. A breezy summer shower pelted the cabbie as he unloaded one large suitcase and a smaller carry-on. Stephen and his parents dashed from the cab to the dry sanctuary of the terminal. Stella, Stephen's mother, was rattling off a list of do's & don'ts faster than Stephen could comprehend them, all the while dabbing at the corners of her eyes with a lace handkerchief.

"And remember, call us the minute you get to Uncle Phillip's."

She then flung herself at Stephen, wrapped her arms around him and sobbed hysterically, "I really can't believe you're leaving already! You just got home. Martin, why are we doing this?" She asked her husband.

Her sentence was cut short by another outburst of crying and Stephen was engulfed in a cloud of Arpege perfume.

"Mom, please!" Stephen choked. "I'm about to miss the train!"

Stephen wiggled out of his mother's grasp. The clamor in Penn Station seemed to be growing as more and more passengers dashed in from the rain. Pools of water formed where travelers were shaking off umbrellas and stomping wet feet.

Stella Moorhouse loosened her grip on her son. "But Stephen, I hate to see you go. You just got home three days ago."

Stella abruptly turned to face her husband. "Martin, I know we thought this was the best thing to do for Stephen's sake, but now that I think about it, sending him to your uncle, when he just graduated from the academy is probably a bad idea."

Martin scowled at his wife. "You know as well as I do that Stephen will have a wonderful time with Uncle Phillip. It's all arranged. We agreed that, under the circumstances, it would be good for Stephen to get away. You couldn't ask for a better place for a young man to spend a summer. Why coop him up in this dirty, crime- ridden city? Anyway, in just a few weeks, we'll be headed up to see him, just as soon as I finish my first draft."

"Well then," Stella snapped, eyes flashing, "I think we should cancel his trip completely. We can all go up together in a few weeks, as a family!"

Stephen held his breath. He could see his newly formed summer plans, his freedom, start to unravel before his eyes.

"No, Mom. I think Dad had a great idea. Just think about all that clean air. I can go hunting and fishing with Uncle Phillip. I can see animals in the wild. This is going to be quite an adventure for me."

"Hunting?" Stella turned with an incredulous look. "Fishing? You grew up in a penthouse in New York City. Wild animals? You don't have a clue of how to survive in the wilderness."

"I won't be living in the wilderness," Stephen countered. "Did you forget where Uncle Phillip lives, the mansion and estate?"

Stephen was actually hoping to be surrounded by Hollywood beauties, rather than wild animals, but he understood that argument would do even less for his cause.

"Stella, we've had this discussion over and over," Martin interrupted. "This is neither the time nor place to rehash this. Stephen has a train to catch. We have tickets to visit him in five weeks and we will all be coming back to the city together."

"I think it's more of a drafty castle than a mansion, if you ask me. It looks like a prop from one of those cheesy movies your uncle keeps cranking out," Stella remarked, still not placated.

Martin glanced at this watch. "It's time to board the train, Stephen. You need to get going."

Stephen breathed a sigh of relief. He wrapped his arms around his mother, planting a big kiss on her cheek. "Love you, mom. I'll miss you both. Please don't worry. I'm excited about my summer in Michigan!"

Stephen turned to his father and shook his hand.

"Thanks for arranging this, Dad. I'll look forward to seeing you and mom in a few weeks. Hope you make good progress on your new play. I'll call you when I arrive."

With a quick wave, Stephen grabbed his bags and headed towards Train 49, the Lake Shore Limited.

Chapter 2

Paulie De Luca straightened his tie in the mirror. At 6'2" and 240 pounds, he was all muscle. Paulie flexed his arms and watched as his suit coat tightened around his biceps. His reflection showed a nose broken at least three times and a thick scar under his chin. This did not bother Paulie. He knew his tough looks were an asset in his profession.

Ever since he was a kid, Paulie wanted to be a 'made man'. After supper, sitting on the porch with his older brother, he would watch the young mob guys go by wearing expensive suits, driving fancy cars and flashing wads of cash.

But it was the women that got to Paulie most of all. The mob guys always had nice women. They were stylish, their nails always done and oh, they smelled so good. These guys seemed to have all the things that were lacking in the De Luca household.

Paulie's mother had run off with a New Jersey truck driver from Hoboken when Paulie was only seven. He lived with his bitter old man and his older brother, Frankie, since then. Now, at 34 years old, Paulie had almost made it, but not quite. He recently had a little problem with the cops that delayed his advancement with the boys.

How was he to know that the storefront he had picked to shake down was a front for the cops? That little mistake had cost the mob a lot of money and delayed Paulie's career path for at least a year. In fact, he was still running around doing favors, trying to get back in the family's good graces.

Paulie went downstairs and made a call.

"Al, how many suits should I pack?" Paulie asked.

"How the hell should I know?" Al screamed into the phone. "You just watch that damn kid. Make sure you keep an eye on him. You get the word to snatch him, and you snatch him. Don't be asking no stupid questions. Take three suits, take six. It don't make no difference. Just keep your eye on the kid."

"Where am I going to?" Paulie asked.

"It don't matter! You go where the kid goes. Paulie, Mr. Sabatini is giving you this opportunity to get right with the guys. Don't blow it. Cuz, guess what? You ain't getting another one, you big muscle bound piece of shit."

Al slammed down the phone. He needed to get Paulie out of town fast. Paulie didn't know how pissed off Mr. Sabatini really was. Paulie's goof had cost Mr. Sabatini big dough. Al always liked Paulie, he had taken him under his wing. By the time Paulie got back, things should have cooled off quite a bit.

Paulie knew it was a big deal. This was his big break. He had a feeling if he did good on this job, he wouldn't have to be doing any more shit jobs on the street. He would probably be in. With that in mind, Paulie packed all his suits and a pair of patent leather shoes, then he tossed in pair of snakeskin shoes just to be safe.

He got a chair from the kitchen and stood so he could reach the ceiling tiles in the living room. Counting to the fourth tile from the corner, he slid it aside, feeling around until his fingers found a hidden box. He took it down and replaced the tile.

The box was dusty. Paulie found a towel and wiped it clean. He opened the box to make sure everything was in place. He was proud of his tool kit. The blindfold was there next to several coils of rope and a pair of brass knuckles. A small revolver was under a false bottom. He took the box and jammed it into his carry on bag.

Paulie reached under his bed and pulled out his most prized possession – a huge book entitled 'Kensington's North American Lepidoptera Field Guide'. The book was at least four inches thick and considered by many to be the premium butterfly identification book in print. Paulie had stolen it from a book store on Thirty-Third Street.

He had become fascinated by butterflies when his 4th grade class had taken a field trip to Central Park and a state biologist had shown the class how to collect the insects. Since that day, Paulie had amassed a huge collection of his own.

He was looking forward to going to a different part of the country, no matter where, to see if he could add some new specimens to his collection. Paulie also packed a bag containing his butterfly net, a small jar of alcohol, some pins and a few wax trays for mounting his collectables. Paulie considered this to be his "secret hobby". No one else knew about his passion.

Penn Station was busy. After ten minutes of walking through the crowds, Al pulled Paulie aside and nodded towards a family huddled together talking near a marble column.

"That's them over there, the kid in the blue shirt. That's the kid you need to keep track of. The kid's name is Stephen Moorhouse and his parents are loaded."

Paulie stared at the kid. The kid's blue shirt was exactly the same color as the Karner Blue butterfly he had been looking at in his Kensington guide just that morning. It was the next butterfly he wanted to hunt down for his collection. Paulie had made a mental note to head up to Saratoga, one of the few remaining places in New York this butterfly could be found, to see if he could find one when he got back. Now this kid shows up wearing a blue shirt exactly the same color. This must be a sign.

Paulie laughed.

"What's so funny?" Al asked.

"Nothing, just something I was thinking about. I better go get a ticket," Paulie said, turning toward a row of ticket booths.

"That's a great idea, Paulie. So where's the ticket gonna take you, genius?" Al glared at him.

Paulie turned back to Al with a befuddled look. "Oh, yeah. Where's the kid headed?"

"How the hell do I know?" Al said, his voice rising over the din of the crowd. Several travelers diverted their path to make room around Al and Paulie.

"You just jump on whatever goddamned train the kid gets on. Then give the conductor twenty bucks and tell him to keep the change. He ain't gonna throw you off the train. Remember, not a word about this to anyone. You understand?"

"I get it, I get it."

"This is just our little conspiracy, just between you and me. Don't go talking like some big shot about what you're gonna do."

Chapter 3

Stephen glanced back to see his parents disappear into the crowd. He walked down the crowded platform, reading the signs. The huge engines on the silver clad trains were making the platform vibrate. He double checked the sign. 'Train 49, Lake Shore Limited'. Stephen felt his pocket to make sure the wad of tickets his uncle had sent him was still there. Stephen joined a line of people handing off their luggage to a porter and boarded the train.

As the train moved out of the terminal, Stephen spotted his parents as they made their way out of the crowd. Fingers pointing, exchanging loud words, they were arguing all the way back to the cab stands.

Stephen walked down the aisle and settled into a seat next to a window. He put his jacket and the sketchbook he always carried with him on the empty seat next to him, along with his carry on bag. He leaned back in his seat and checked his watch. Three forty five, right on time.

It had been his idea to take the train. Now that school was over, he had the whole summer to himself. A train ride to Michigan seemed exciting and adventurous. He had spent all of his life in New York City except for the occasional trip to Europe with his Mother and Father. This would be a great experience to see some of the country side, and besides, he needed to get away.

It would be nineteen hours before the train rolled into Chicago, so Stephen had brought a few things to keep him busy. He had his sketchbook, of course, along with a few magazines, a book and a "Welcome To RISD" pamphlet. He would be starting classes at the Rhode Island School of Design in the fall and he had wanted to read up on the school before he got there.

Al and Paulie watched as the kid got on the train.

"Good luck, Paulie," Al said, slapping him on the back. "Don't disappoint the boys on this one."

Paulie walked to the train car, turned to wave at Al, and disappeared into the doorway. Paulie walked down the aisle, spotted Stephen and took a seat a few rows in front. Thankfully, Al had given him a newspaper and every five or ten minutes, Paulie would peer over the top to make sure his "little butterfly" was still in the same place.

About five o'clock Stephen tossed down the RISD pamphlet. He pulled a wrinkled envelope from his pocket and took out a letter. He had read the letter so many times, he could recite it by heart. Jill, his girlfriend for three years, wrote how she was not going to be backpacking though Europe with him for the summer, as planned. She explained how she had met another guy, Ralph, and was going to be traveling in Europe with him this summer instead.

As he got to the part where Jill wrote she hoped he would understand and that she still wanted to be friends, Stephen stopped, folding up the letter and sticking it back into his pocket. He picked up his sketchbook.

As long as Stephen could remember, he was constantly sketching. He knew the train would be an excellent place to do some character studies, wondering if passengers in New York would look the same as passengers in Chicago.

"Excuse me, can I take a look at your magazine?" a man sitting in the aisle seat asked him.

"Sure," Stephen replied, tossing the periodical over. A close-up picture of a giant shark's head was on the cover and the magazine featured a story about the new movie 'Jaws' that had just come out along with information about all the other summer block buster movies. Stephen wondered if there was a movie theater where he was going.

He began to sketch. His car was about one-third full. Most of the travelers appeared to be businessmen. There were a few families and one or two single women traveling alone, but Stephen saw mostly businessmen in suits. He occupied the next hour sketching the passengers around him.

"Here's your magazine back, thank you. Oh, that's quite good!"

Stephen glanced up.

A short, pudgy man, wearing an obvious toupee, sat in the aisle seat.

"I hope you don't mind, but I've been watching you draw," the man said, leaning over an empty seat between them. "You're quite accomplished. Say, I'm heading to the dining car for a cup of coffee, maybe grab something to eat. Care to join me? Maybe stretch your legs a little?"

"Sounds like a good idea."

The pudgy man rose from his seat and motioned for Stephen to follow.

Walking down the aisle, the man turned to Stephen, "I'm Dominick, but everyone calls me Dom."

"I'm Stephen. Nice to meet you, Dom."

They walked through another passenger car on their way to the dining car.

A waiter appeared and Dom ordered two coffees.

"So, Stephen, what puts you on a train headed for Chicago? I thought young people only flew these days," Dom inquired.

"They do if they're in a hurry. I'd rather take some time and see some of the country. And after watching the news on TV about the Eastern flight 66 crash, I'm glad I decided to take the train. I'm headed to Chicago first, then picking up a train to Milwaukee and then taking a bus to northern Michigan."

"That's quite a trip." Dom said, "So what's in Michigan? Must be a girl, eh?" he smiled.

Stephen felt a twinge and Dom could see he had struck a nerve.

"No, I'm staying at my uncle's house in Upper Michigan for the summer."

Back in the passenger car, Paulie glanced over the top of his newspaper. What the hell? Two empty seats greeted his gaze. The seats where Stephen and the fat guy with the cheap toupee had been sitting in were now empty.

Paulie stood up and looked around. He frantically eyed the train car. Where was the little bastard? He had to be on the train somewhere. Was he in the restroom? Maybe, but not likely since the guy sitting next to him was gone too. The dining car? Paulie glanced at this watch. Five fifteen, yeah, almost dinner time. They had better be in the damn dining car!

Stephen could see the waiter heading their way with two cups of coffee on his tray. A large swarthy man in a suit that seemed way too tight came barreling down the aisle and nearly pushed the waiter over.

The waiter stumbled backwards, then to the side. He leaned over to regain his balance as he steadied himself and the tray.

The swarthy man threw himself into a booth on the other side of the aisle. He buried his face in a newspaper and shot a quick glance at the booth Stephen and Dom were sitting in.

The waiter settled himself in front of Stephen and Dom's table and set down two white porcelain mugs filled with steaming black coffee. Not a drop had spilled.

"Nice foot work!" Stephen commented.

The waiter stammered a gruff "hmmmmph", picked up his empty tray and headed to the end of the dining car. Midway down the aisle Paulie waved the waiter over.

"Hey, get me a cup of coffee."

The waiter scowled. For a moment Stephen thought the tray was coming straight down on the big guys head.

"Sugar?" Dom asked.

"Sure." Stephen tore open a packet and poured it into his coffee.

"How long have you been drawing?" Dom asked.

"As long as I can remember, I take my sketchbook everywhere."

"Your sketches really capture your subjects. Looks like you've drawn everyone in our car, including me."

"I hope you don't mind," Stephen responded.

"No, not at all. Are you in art school?"

"I just graduated from Bastion Heights Academy. I'm headed to the Rhode Island School of Design in the fall. I can't wait. That's why I'm drawing on this trip. I figure traveling by train would provide a much better place to do some character studies than on an airplane and I wanted to see some of the country, too."

"Bastion Heights! I'm very impressed," Dom said. "If you attended Bastion, you must be a very well-connected young man. Your parents must be somewhat famous. Anyone I've heard of?"

Stephen grinned.

"Not everyone from Bastion is from a famous family. But you would probably know my mother, Stella Moorhouse and my father is..."

"Stella Moorhouse from the game show 'What's My Story'?" Dom interrupted. Stephen laughed.

"Yes, that would be her."

Stephen knew his mother would not be happy to hear that response. Now days she prided herself on her numerous charity works. She would rather have been associated with her movie credits ten years earlier, than to be known from that silly game show. Stephen had heard her rant and rave about this topic on many occasions.

"So that means your father is the up and coming Broadway playwright, Martin Moorhouse, as in 'The Nuremburg Secrets', right?"

"That would be him," Stephen agreed.

"I saw that play last year and I thought it was brilliant," Dom said. "Very thought provoking."

Stephen and Dominick passed the time talking about their destinations, trading reasons why they thought the train was better than flying.

"I was supposed to be backpacking in Europe with my girlfriend," Stephen said. "But she sort of dumped me at the last minute and now I'm on my way to visit my uncle for the summer."

"I'm sorry to hear that, Stephen. I know it's rough being dumped by a woman. We've all been there, that's for sure. A handsome lad like yourself should spring back quickly," Dom remarked. "But surely northern Michigan will be pretty sparse in the bevy of beautiful women department, compared to New York City, right?"

"You might be surprised. My uncle is a Hollywood director and I'm hoping his estate is teeming with actresses."

"No kidding? So, who's your uncle?"

"Phillip Kahle."

"Oh, yes. I loved his horror movies from a few years ago. Very campy!"

After the second cup of coffee, Dominick suggested they order some dinner.

Halfway through the meal, Dom asked Stephen, "See that man sitting over there who almost knocked over the waiter?"

Stephen looked, then reached down and grabbed his sketch book. He flipped open several pages and asked, "This guy?"

"Yes, that's the guy. You've captured him quite nicely. Do you know him?"

"No, why would you think I know him?" Stephen asked.

"Actually, no reason, but he seems to be staring at us a little more than normal. Probably nothing, I just was wondering. It seemed a little odd, that's all."

Stephen thought he was probably staring at Dom's hair piece, but said instead, "No, I've never seen him before. I'm sure he's just bored and looking around the coach. There's nothing special about me to be looking at."

With dinner finished, the waiter cleared their table and Stephen and Dom returned to the passenger car.

The evening was spent watching the lights of the countryside pass by, with pauses interrupted by talk of art school, business, and sports.

Around eleven thirty, Stephen excused himself for the night, heading to the view liner roomette his uncle had reserved. Dom said goodnight indicating he was going to sleep in the passenger car.

Paulie was fighting to stay awake when he noticed the kid get up and move past him. Trying not to look too obvious, he rose and followed Stephen from a distance. Paulie followed as Stephen walked through the next passenger car, the dining car and entered the sleeper coach section. Dom observed what was transpiring and decided to get up and follow them both.

Since he hadn't booked any sleeping accommodations, Paulie figured the best place to keep on eye on the kid was in the nearest passenger car to the sleeper coach. As Paulie returned through the dining car, he passed Dom in the aisle, glaring at him.

Paulie entered the passenger car and found an empty seat close to the door. He tossed his hat in the seat next to him, took off his suit coat and draped it over himself like a blanket.

Dom followed from a distance, picking a seat four rows behind and sat down. Dom wanted to keep an eye on that big goon who seemed to be following Stephen.

Stephen entered the sleeper car. He stepped in and looked around. Not bad, he thought. The room was small, about three and a half feet by seven. It had an upper berth and two reclining seats that looked like they could be made into a bed, if necessary. There was a small toilet and sink with a shower area down the hall. Stephen popped up a little table which faced a window with curtains and sat in one of the reclining seats. He stared out the window as the countryside passed by.

Stephen took out Jill's letter and started to read it again. He got half way through and crumpled the letter up in a ball. Why dwell on the past, he thought. This trip is the start of a brand new future. He tossed it into the garbage can.

After twenty minutes, Stephen was getting tired. He got ready for bed, pulling the window curtains closed and jumped up into the berth. Stephen fell asleep to the clicking sounds of the rails moving rhythmically beneath him.

The next morning, Stephen stirred as the rising sun brightened the window behind the curtains. At first he was confused as to where he was. He had been dreaming about seeing Jill walking down a street in Paris with another guy. In the dream, as he approached them, Jill pointed to Stephen and started to laugh.

It was then he had stirred himself awake. He glanced out at the passing landscape and tried to get into a happier mood. Stephen dressed quickly and decided to see if Dom would like to have a cup of coffee or some breakfast. Maybe conversation with his new friend would help to cheer him up.

Stephen carefully navigated the distance from the sleeper to the adjoining passenger car. He gave a start as he saw the big guy in the suit, sleeping next to the door. Stephen saw Dom sitting a few rows behind him. Dom put his finger to his lips motioning towards the dining car. Stephen nodded and turned around. Walking quietly past the sleeping Paulie, Dom noticed a huge book, with pictures of butterflies, open on his lap.

Seated in the dining car, Dom briefed Stephen on what had happened during the night.

Dom asked, "Why would this guy get up and go to the sleeper coach at the same time you did, then turn around and park himself in the car closer to you, if he wasn't following you?"

"Maybe he just wanted a quieter place to sleep?"

"Well, there were fewer people in that car," Dom agreed.

"That's got to be it. Why would anyone want to be following me?"

Dom glanced at the entrance to the dining car.

"Don't look now, but guess who just walked in."

Paulie walked by trying not to look at Stephen. It was evident he had just woken up. His hair was a mess. Paulie's face showed an overnight growth of whiskers and his suit was a mass of wrinkles. As Paulie walked in, Stephen turned his face to the window.

The landscape rushing past was pale grey with a soft mist covering farm fields intersected by small thickets of woods. Dom and Stephen ordered breakfast.

Around nine thirty, the Lake Shore Limited came around a bend and the sky-scrapers of downtown Chicago could be seen in the far distance.

"It looks like we're getting into Chicago," Stephen said to Dom. "Thanks for making the time go by quickly and thanks for watching out for me."

"I enjoyed meeting you, Stephen. Keep your eyes peeled, if you know what I mean. Once you get to the station, you should call your father and let him know what's been happening."

The train jerked to a stop. Paulie finished his coffee as he watched Stephen get up and head out of the dining car.

Chapter 4

Chicago's Union Station had the look of being built in the early 1900's. Stephen gazed up at the arched ceiling of the great hall, at least one hundred feet above his head. Corinthian columns stood on polished marble floors. Since it was only ten o'clock in the morning, and his train to Milwaukee didn't leave till five, Stephen decided to take advantage of the time and spend the day at the Art Institute.

He stored his bags in a locker and pulled out a map he had brought with him from New York. Thinking about calling his father, Stephen walked over to a pay phone. He hesitated. Since this was his first real trip away by himself, it would not look good if he needed to call home in a panic over some wild story about being followed by a stranger. He decided to wait and see if anything else happened. He could always tell Uncle Phillip, once he got to Michigan.

The sky was clear as he headed down Jackson Street towards Michigan Avenue. It was a little more than a mile and it felt good to be walking outside after being cooped up on the train for so long. Before he knew it, Stephen was climbing the steps to The Art Institute, with its signature giant green patina lions elegantly standing guard on either side.

Paulie was following a block behind. He almost lost track of Stephen when, what appeared to be a swamp Metalmark butterfly, flitted by. Without thinking, Paulie turned and followed the butterfly a few steps before losing it into some bushes. Could that really have been a Metalmark? Paulie chalked it up to wishful thinking, because Metalmarks were way too rare, and he didn't notice any swamp thistle growing in the middle of Chicago's busy metropolis.

Stephen picked up a display pamphlet and strolled up the stairs to Gunsaulus Hall. Japanese collections lined the corridor but Stephen hardly glanced at them. As he approached McKinlock Court, Stephen paused to check out a display of sketches by Thomas Addison Richards. A sign explained that Richards was an artist who traveled the south in the 1800s. Stephen thought how excited Jill would be to hear about his visit to the museum. Jill loved art as much as Stephen. A crushing reality hit him as he remembered that he would not be having any more discussions with her.

He stepped back to get a better view. Out of the corner of his eye, he saw someone enter the gallery. It was the same big guy from the train. Stephen recognized the wrinkled suit. They made eye contact for a fleeting second as the burly man entered the gallery. The man quickly turned and walked over to examine a collection of paintings on the other side of the room.

Stephen's heart began to beat faster. He tried to calculate what the odds would be that this guy would happen to take the same train from New York to Chicago, have a fellow passenger suspicious of him, and then have him show up in the same gallery of the museum. He didn't like the odds.

Stephen turned into the sculpture room located to the right of McKinlock Court. As he entered the room he thought, I need to find out once and for all if this guy is following me.

Stephen jogged halfway through the court and quickly ducked behind a statue that looked to be a cross between a man in a suit of armor and some kind of bionic robot. He held his breath pressing himself tightly behind the big sculpture. He counted off the seconds, "thousand one, thousand two, thousand three." Stephen listened but did not hear anyone pass by. After what seemed like half an hour, he slowly peered out into the gallery. The gallery was empty.

He slipped quietly from behind the statue and started to walk around the sculpture court. Stephen breathed a sigh of relief and thought about Dom. His crazy talk, combined with traveling alone for the first time, must have worked together to create a feeling of paranoia. Stephen resolved to calm down and enjoy the rest of the exhibits. He consulted the map and headed towards Rubloff Auditorium.

Paulie panicked when he had run straight into the kid. That encounter was way too close. He did not want to be recognized or discovered following his prey. The long open hallways did not provide ideal conditions for tailing someone. Paulie decided to head back to the train depot in hopes that the kid returned through the same Jackson Street entrance he left from.

By four o'clock, Stephen had seen most of The Art Institute and had enjoyed a quick lunch. He decided it was time to get back to Union Station. On the walk back, Stephen reviewed all of the great art he had experienced. Periodically he glanced behind him to make sure no one was following him.

Paulie was in a perfect position to see Stephen enter Union Station. He watched as Stephen retrieved his bags and headed for No. 339, the Hiawatha Service. Still spooked from his face to face encounter, Paulie was determined not to get too close again.

He waited several minutes after Stephen got on the train before attempting to board. Paulie approached the train.

"Ticket, please."

A burly conductor held out his hand. Paulie folded over a twenty dollar bill.

"Here you go, buddy. Keep the change," Paulie said, as he walked past the man.

"Hold it, Mister. You gotta have a ticket. Ticket window's over there." The conductor indicated with a nod.

Paulie was in a panic. He didn't want the train to leave without him. What would he tell Al. He ran over to the ticket booth.

"I need a ticket for that train," Paulie said, pointing to the 339.

"What is your destination, sir? Are you going to Milwaukee?"

"Yeah, that's it. Give me a ticket to Milwaukee."

Paulie grabbed the ticket, rushed back to the conductor, shoved the ticket in his hand and climbed onto the train. He grabbed the first seat he could find and decided to worry about spotting Stephen when they got to Milwaukee.

About quarter to seven, the Hiawatha Service pulled into the Milwaukee Station. Stephen grabbed his bags and headed to the lobby. There was a two hour wait which passed quickly and around nine o'clock Stephen boarded a bus for the Upper Michigan city of Escanaba. Stephen took a window seat.

The Milwaukee Depot was not nearly as crowded as Chicago's Union Station. Paulie stayed in the shadows and thought he would have a much easier time boarding the same bus Stephen got on. As a precaution, Paulie removed his hat and suit coat and combed his hair so his part was on the opposite side. Again, he waited to board the bus a few minutes after Stephen. Paulie took a seat in the front.

Stephen sat down and tried to stay awake. It had been a long day and he had nearly nodded off before the bus even pulled out of the terminal. He tried to concentrate on the landscape rolling by the window and noticed that as the cities were getting smaller, they were also further apart. Rural landscapes became the norm.

Around midnight, Stephen tried to get some sleep. He wasn't expected to arrive in Escanaba until sometime around three thirty and he didn't want to be dead tired when Uncle Phillip picked him up.

Paulie was also having a hard time staying awake. It was getting hot on the bus. Since he didn't know where Stephen was headed, he needed to be awake to see every passenger depart at each stop.

As the cities disappeared, Paulie started feeling uneasy. He watched as thick forests replaced rolling farmlands. Several times he saw deer standing along the highway. The familiar city sounds he experienced in Milwaukee were replaced by silence. He was feeling very uncomfortable. Just after two o'clock, the bus pulled into Menominee and three passengers got off. Paulie slept soundly through the stop.

As the bus pulled out of the small depot, Paulie rubbed his eyes and snapped awake. He jumped to his feet and scanned the bus. He breathed a sigh of relief when he spotted Stephen, leaning against the window, fast asleep. Paulie vowed to stay awake for the rest of the trip, no matter how long it took.

Chapter 5

It was four fifteen when the bus pulled into the Escanaba bus depot. Not so much a bus depot really, but a small room tacked on to a bowling alley. Two bars and a diner were conveniently located across the street, but at this time of morning, everything was closed. A lonely cab was parked just across from the bowling alley.

Stephen joined four other passengers as they stumbled out of the bus, all half awake. He stepped into the bright fluorescently lit room and looked around for his uncle. It had been several years since he had seen Uncle Phillip during a brief visit to New York City, but Stephen didn't think he would have any trouble recognizing him again.

Just as he had determined none of the people in the bus terminal could possibly be him, the door swung open and Stephen recognized the man walking in.

Uncle Phillip stood 6'2" with closely trimmed blond hair. He sported a California tan, which made him stand out in the midst of the pale mid-westerners around him. Stephen remembered him as being very outgoing and he always seemed to have smile on his face. Stephen strode up to him.

"Hello, Uncle Phillip."

Phillip took a second to respond.

"Stephen, is that you? My, how you've grown. I was looking for someone much shorter! It's been about three years, yes?"

Stephen remembered his uncle's slight German accent.

"Yes, I think it has been that long."

Phillip reached down, "Let me help you with your things."

Phillip grabbed one of Stephen's bags and they walked to the car. He opened the trunk of a Porsche and tossed in the bag.

"Tonight we stay at the House of Ludington Hotel. I think you will like it. It's on Lake Michigan. I knew you would be tired, so I thought it would be best that we didn't drive the 120 miles to Grand View this late. Too many deer," Phillip gave a laugh, "and I drive too fast in this fancy car."

Paulie ran over to the waiting cab.

"Where to, Mister?" the cabbie asked.

"Follow that Porsche".

Stephen jumped into the car and froze. "Uncle Phillip, see that man talking to the cabbie?"

"Yes."

"You won't believe this, but I think he's been following me this whole trip. All the way from Penn Station."

"Stephen, is that so?" Phillip asked with a look of disbelief on his face.

"No, I mean it. Even another person I met on the train thought so and that was before we even arrived in Chicago. He followed me when I walked to the Art Institute and now he's here in Escanaba."

"Well, I guess it could be," Phillip said, noticing his look had upset his nephew. "But, we do get visitors from all over the world to our beautiful Upper Peninsula every now and then." Phillip paused for a moment. "Is there a reason why someone would be following you?"

Stephen thought for a moment, "Well, no..."

"What I think is that you must be very tired."

"I am."

"Okay, so you get a good night's sleep tonight. Tomorrow we'll keep a watch out for anyone following us back to the house. What do you think of that idea?"

"That sounds good," Stephen was reassured by his Uncle's words.

Phillip put the car in gear and pulled out of the parking lot. The cab slowly followed through the darkness, keeping a discrete distance.

Chapter 6

The next morning Paulie was already sitting in a rental car when Stephen and his uncle finished breakfast and pulled out.

It was a beautiful morning with a clear blue sky and the temperature was a brisk sixty seven degrees. Paulie watched as Phillip walked Stephen across the street to the lakefront.

"There's much history in this area," Phillip said. "I can imagine French explorers paddling their canoes in this bay, with Indians watching from the forests."

On the drive out of town, Phillip pointed out Little Bay De Noc.

"The fishing is very good here. We should go sometime," Phillip declared.

Remembering Stephen's concern from the night before, Phillip periodically glanced into the rear view mirror to see if anyone was following them. He didn't notice anything unusual.

"Are you ready to spend your summer in the wilds of Upper Michigan?" Uncle Phillip asked. "I hope you don't get bored. It's not like the city, there really isn't so much to do."

"I've brought my sketchbook and Dad told me about your huge library and the theater room. I'm sure I can keep busy. Do you get any visitors from Hollywood?" Stephen asked, remembering his dream of being surrounded by actresses.

"Now and then, but most of my Hollywood friends find the area too isolated and out of the way."

Stephen was a little discouraged.

"Did you hear about my girlfriend?" Stephen asked.

"Yes, your father told what happened when we talked about your trip to visit me. Women, very difficult. Don't I know," Phillip shook his head. "But we get on with things and live to see another day. I think you staying here with me will help, right?"

Stephen nodded, "That's for sure. This was a great idea".

After an hour of driving, Stephen watched as the forest got thicker. The green leaves of maple and beech were replaced by dark green needles of fir and pine. Stephen could actually smell a fresh pine scent seeping into the car. Small streams and bogs appeared on both sides of the road.

Stephen turned to his uncle.

"How did you end up here in northern Michigan? It seems pretty remote."

Uncle Phillip laughed, "Good question. That's the same thing my California friends ask me. But to answer your question, I was born in Germany, in the Kahle Forest area, which was named after our family."

"Did it look like this?" Stephen asked.

"Yes, the land was very similar."

"What made you come to the states?

"Much luck, Stephen."

"What do you mean?"

"Well, when I was in my late twenties, I had made a few low budget pictures in Germany that got noticed by some Americans when they were screened in France. From that, I was asked to direct a small project in Hollywood."

"Did you like it when you first came to the states?"

"Oh my, can you imagine? A young man, working in Germany one day and then in California, the next. The first few years in California were exciting, but after five years, not so much. I missed my homeland and the forests. I longed for a quiet retreat. Something similar to where I was raised."

"So how did you find this area?"

"At the time, I was a fan of Hemingway's books, yes?" He had written a story called 'Big Two-Hearted River' that was about this area. I came to check it out. Then I feel like I'm back in Germany. So I buy some land."

"Is your place near that river?"

"Only about fifty miles away. We need to go sometime and I can show you."

"How long do you stay when you come up here?"

"That depends on how busy I am with my movies. I try to get here the first part of June and stay until the end of September. Usually I have to make a trip or two back to Los Angeles to keep up with business."

Phillip pointed to a sign.

"Blaney Park. We turn here. Only forty miles to go. I'm sure you are ready to end your journey."

"It will be nice to stop living out of a suitcase," Stephen agreed.

Phillip glanced up at the rear view mirror. He was careful not to be too obvious and catch Stephen's attention. A blue Ford had left Escanaba when they did and followed them, turn for turn. Phillip had purposely sped up and slowed down to see how the car behind would react. The blue Ford had always remained about the same distance behind, no matter what speed Phillip was traveling.

If Stephen had not mentioned the possibility of being followed, Phillip wasn't sure he would have noticed this car.

Trying to sound casual, Phillip asked, "Stephen, who else knew you were coming to visit me this summer besides your parents?"

"Let me think. My three best friends at Bastion Academy. They gave me a hard time about spending my summer in the woods. Two nights before I left, Mom and Dad had a cocktail party and we also talked about my trip then."

"That must have been nice. Who was there?" Uncle Phillip asked casually.

"Let's see. My Dad's literary agent, Mr. Plotnick and his wife. The couple that live upstairs. They had just returned home from Europe so they wanted to tell us all about their trip. There was also another couple I didn't really know. I'm not sure why they were at the party, but I think their names were Beach. Mrs. Beach had a little too much to drink and Mr. Beach just sat there. He was a quiet guy, he didn't say too much."

Uncle Phillip thought for a while. "Well, I want you to know I'm very happy you decided to spend your summer with me. When did you come up with this idea?"

"About a week before school got out, Dad called and said he had a great idea. When he told me what it was, I thought it sounded like a lot of fun."

They drove passed a sign welcoming them to the Seney Wildlife Refuge boundary when Stephen spotted something running next to the road.

"What is that?" Stephen said, pointing out the window.

"Let's see, is it a coyote? No too big," Phillip said as he slowed the car down to a crawl. "Too big for a coyote means that's a timberwolf."

"A wolf?"

"I told you we were in the middle of nowhere!" Uncle Phil answered, with a note of pride in his voice.

Chapter 7

It wasn't hot, but Paulie was sweating. Nothing felt right about this job. If he had known he was headed to Hicksville, in the middle of a million damn trees, he would have never accepted this worthless job.

Ever since Milwaukee, the roads and towns got smaller and smaller and the woods got bigger and darker. He was never afraid walking the streets and parks of New York City alone at night, but this was something else. It was hard to concentrate on not being spotted by the Porsche. Paulie thought of Al and Mr. Sabatini. He hammered the steering wheel with his hand and hollered, "Those idiots better give me a good job after this bullshit."

Phillip crested a hill and pointed.

"Take a look at that sign. We're almost home."

The sign read 'Welcome to Grand View, Population 478'. Phillip drove a short distance over the hill and without slowing down, made a quick left turn onto Pine Ridge Road. The turn was fast and unexpected. Stephen lurched over to the right and hit his shoulder hard on the passenger door.

"Whoa, this car really corners! Warn me next time, will you?" He laughed.

"Sorry about that. I forgot I had a passenger." Phillip slowed the car and watched through the rear view mirror as the blue Ford continued straight ahead, unaware of their quick exit. Uncle Phillip smiled.

"Only two more miles, Stephen. Then we're home."

Paulie's rental car crested the hill. He read the sign. Population 478! You've got to be kidding me, Paulie thought. There's more people living in my building than in this whole damn town!

Paulie stared at the road ahead of him. There was no sign of the Porsche. What the hell? All Paulie could see were several billboards advertising a bar, a few restaurants, and one motel.

Pine Ridge Road was somewhat misleading since it was only a narrow gravel path through the woods. After two miles they came to a gentle curve and the Porsche pulled up to the front of a huge gate. A large brass sign mounted to a fieldstone wall read Cliffside Manor. Phillip pushed a button and the gate quietly swung open. They had driven past a few cars parked a block or two before the gate and several people had been milling around. Phillip ignored them and they seemed to ignore him, too. No one attempted to enter when the gate opened.

"Who are they?" Stephen asked.

"Those guys are a big pain in my ass," Phillip said, his face darkening. "I'll tell you all about them sometime when Britt's not around."

As the car rounded a corner, a huge English Tudor mansion came into view. Stephen recognized it immediately. It looked exactly like the mansion in his Uncle's movie, 'Attack of the Piltdown Man'.

Behind the house, set off to the left, was a smaller dwelling, designed in the same style. Uncle Phillip pulled up to the massive front door and stopped the car. Stephen jumped out and grabbed his bags. Uncle Phillip held the door open as they entered the mansion.

The foyer was open and extended up three stories. To the right was what looked to be an oak paneled office. On the left was a very comfortable lounge, complete with a ten point buck mounted over a fireplace, and an eight foot stuffed brown bear standing in a corner.

"That's the trophy room," Uncle Phillip said, as he walked to the door of the office.

"That's quite a bear," Stephen remarked.

"I've got an even bigger one somewhere in storage," Uncle Phillip replied. Phillip called down the hallway, "Jeanette, we're back."

A young woman in her early 20's walked out of the office. "And this must be Stephen", she said, extending her hand. "I'm Jeanette St. Jacques, your uncle's personal assistant. Very nice to meet you."

Stephen took her hand, "Nice to meet you, too." Stephen liked what he saw. Maybe not a Hollywood starlet, he thought, but pretty close.

Jeanette was about 5'6", with an athletic frame. She had straight black hair that went down over her shoulders, blue eyes and high cheekbones.

Uncle Phillip said, "Stephen, welcome to Cliffside Manor. Please make yourself at home. I have a long distance call in thirty minutes I have to prepare for. I'll let Jeanette show you around. I'm sure you won't mind. We can all meet in the dinning room for lunch in a couple of hours."

Stephen took another look at Jeanette. "That's fine, Uncle Phillip. Not a problem."

Jeanette grabbed Stephen's carry on bag. "Let me give you a quick tour while I show you where you will be staying."

"Okay, that would be nice."

"Let's start in this first downstairs room, the trophy room. Mr. Kahle's decorated it in a very northern Michigan style with the deer head and bear. He's not a hunter, but he wanted a very rustic comfortable room. Most of his relaxing time is spent in here."

"I like the stone fireplace," Stephen added.

"It comes in very handy since we don't get many warm days around here," Jeanette said. "As you will see, this mansion is built on a cliff that rises three hundred feet above Lake Superior. Superior is the great lakes deepest lake so it never warms up in the summer which makes the breezes very cool. There are spectacular views from every room in the back of the mansion."

"I noticed how cool it was when I got out of the car."

"Get used to it. It's like that almost every day."

"My office is over here. You have to walk through my office to get to your uncle's. I'm both his assistant and his gate keeper," Jeanette said with a laugh. "Even though he comes up here to get away, he works almost every day."

"What kind of work?" Stephen inquired.

"Script writing, mostly. But there are a lot of business things to take care of when doing a picture."

Jeanette pointed, "Down that hall and to the left is the dinning room and kitchen. Running along the back of the house is a large glassed-in area we call the conservatory."

Jeanette was marching down hallways pointing out various rooms and architectural features. Clearly she had conducted this tour many times before. Lugging his suitcase, Stephen was struggling to keep up.

"Do you know where the design of Cliffside Manor came from?" Jeanette asked.

"It looks just like the house in Attack of the Piltdown Man."

"Very good, Stephen. I'm impressed. That was the third movie he produced in Hollywood and it turned out to be very profitable. Because of that, it was possible to build this estate. Your Uncle thought it would be fun to design this house just like the mansion in the movie." Jeanette stopped to let Stephen catch up.

"Okay, now for the second floor."

True to the design, the staircase looked old and somewhat sinister.

"Mr. Kahle's bedroom suite is at the far end of this hall. My room is here and at this end there are four guest suites. You're staying in suite number three."

Rich, dark mahogany covered the walls of the hall. As far as Stephen was concerned, all that was missing from the hallways were the cobwebs he remembered from the spooky mansion in the movie.

Jeanette swung open the door to his room. Stephen's suite was large and consisted of a bedroom, a bathroom, and a small living room/study area. Large windows faced manicured grounds which ran to the edge of a cliff. A low stone wall ran along the cliff's edge.

Jeanette and Stephen walked to the windows. The waves of Lake Superior could be seen lapping the shore hundreds of feet below.

"This is spectacular!" Stephen marveled. "I feel dizzy just looking at such a drop."

"Set your bags down and I'll show you the third floor," Jeanette said.

On the way upstairs, Stephen asked, "How long have you worked for my uncle?"

"I've been working here at Cliffside Manor ever since I was 16, doing one job or another. Two years ago I got the personal assistant job and I love it. I get to meet many famous Hollywood types, directors, producers, and actors."

Stephen asked, "I noticed another house sitting to the left and behind the mansion. What's that for, more guests?"

For a brief second a cloud crossed Jeanette's face.

"No, that's a cottage where your uncle's friend, Britt Adolfson, the Swedish actress, lives. She starred in many of his movies."

"Oh, Britt. Yes, Uncle Phillip mentioned her when he visited us a few years ago. Has she been in any movies recently?"

"I don't think she's very interested in acting these days. Your Uncle keeps asking her to go with him on his trips back to Hollywood, but she hardly ever does."

"It does seem very relaxing here," Stephen mentioned.

Jeanette stopped at the top of the stairs. "The main rooms on the third floor are the billiards room, the library, and the theater where we screen movies. There are also two additional guest rooms, a gym and along the back is a terrace that overlooks Lake Superior."

"You have a gym?" Stephen asked.

"Yes, but nobody ever uses it, except for our guard. He wanted a place where he could work out with his weights and punching bag, so Mr. Kahle set up a room for him."

"A guard?"

"Yes, we have a guard that lives on the property." Jeanette directed Stephen into the library. "You have to see this room. I love the floor to ceiling windows and the books, of course."

Stephen surveyed the room with its leather armchairs, Tiffany lamps, and the spectacular view of the lake.

Jeanette continued, "It's nice to spend rainy days here getting lost in a book."

"Yes, this would be the perfect place to hibernate."

As they left the library, Jeanette closed the heavy oak doors and walked down to the end of the hallway.

"This is the theater room. Your uncle has equipped this room with a large projection screen that drops from the ceiling, a seating area with twenty theater seats, a bar area, and a huge selection of movie reels. He's got all the movies he produced and directed, of course, but he's also very proud of his collection of black and white movie reels. I think they are his favorites."

Stephen walked around the room thinking how great it must be to have your own movie theater.

"I hope you like scary movies, Stephen, because your uncle's collection is one of the best. I guess that's where he gets his inspiration from."

They left the theater and walked back down to the second level to Stephen's room.

"That's the tour. Why don't you take some time to relax, put your things away and meet your uncle downstairs in an hour or so for lunch."

Stephen watched as Jeanette left his room. He had a feeling this was going to be a very special summer. Stephen sat on the bed and looked around his suite. He had to hand it to Uncle Phillip. The dark wood, the antiques, everything in the room could have been taken directly from a movie set.

Stephen walked to the far side of the room and opened two windows. A smell of fresh pine filled the air. He could hear the rhythmic sound of Lake Superior's pounding surf. I'm going to love sleeping with that sound in the background, Stephen thought to himself. He unpacked his bags and stored his belongings in the big closet and numerous drawers in the antique dresser. He stretched out on the bed and quickly fell asleep.

Once again, he dreamed of Jill. This time he was sitting on a large boulder next to a waterfall. In his dream he was calling her name. Jill approached him from a watery mist and put her hand softly on his shoulder. He turned around and they were embracing. He was thrilled that they were together again.

Stephen woke up and glanced around. He was alone in the room. His sudden joy evaporated like the dream. Rubbing his eyes and yawning, Stephen got up and straightened the comforter on the bed. He wondered if he would ever reach a point when Jill was either not on his mind or surfacing in his subconscious. Stephen glanced at the clock on the nightstand. It was seven minutes past noon. He splashed some water on his face, combed his hair and headed downstairs.

As he entered the dining room, he saw his uncle was sitting next to a beautiful blonde. Stephen presumed she was Britt. They were deep in conversation. As soon as Stephen entered the room Uncle Phillip stood up and introduced him.

"Britt, this is my nephew, from New York City. As I mentioned, he will be spending the summer here with us before heading back east to attend art school in the fall."

"Stephen, so nice to finally meet you. Did you have a nice nap?" Britt rose from the table and gave him a big hug.

Stephen was not prepared for this. Britt's hair was in his face. It smelled wonderful and felt soft. During her embrace, she pressed her body snuggly into his. Stephen stood still, his arms hanging straight down at his sides. Finally, Britt let go and Uncle Phillip motioned for Stephen to take a seat at the table.

Still somewhat unnerved, Stephen replied, "Yes, I fell asleep right away. My room is spectacular and I could hear the waves from the lake."

Jeanette entered the room and sat at the table across from Uncle Phillip. A short grey haired woman wearing an apron entered the dining room and placed bowls of homemade vegetable soup in front of everyone.

"Stephen, I'd like you to meet Cora Ingebritzen," Phillip introduced. "She's the best cook you could ever find. I can thank her personally for adding two inches to my waistline." Everyone laughed.

As they ate, Stephen couldn't help staring at Britt. He remembered seeing her in his Uncle's movies years ago, but seeing her in person was another thing all together. She looked a little older but her sensuality had only increased. She had a beautiful face with a very fair complexion. Her hair was platinum blond and curly. She was voluptuous and the low cut peasant blouse she was wearing did nothing to hide her curves. When she spoke, she still had a slight Swedish accent. This, combined with her feminine ways, proved to be a mesmerizing package to Stephen, and to most men who got the chance to meet her, he thought. Jeanette glanced up at Stephen but quickly returned her gaze to her soup.

"Stephen, when you were at the main gate, did you see any members of my fan club?" Britt asked with a laugh.

Uncle Phillip responded, "Hardly a fan club, darling. I wish you would take them a little more seriously. I don't think you completely understand the hunting culture of this area."

Britt's thick lips pouted.

"Innocent, beautiful creatures were not put on this world to be slaughtered for someone's amusement. Don't these savages realize we have grocery stores now for food?"

Britt slammed her hand onto the table. "This endless killing cycle is senseless and completely unnecessary."

Uncle Phillip looked at Stephen.

"As you can see, Stephen, Britt is an animal advocate. She has riled up the local hunting community with her outspoken commentary. For some reason, she fails to understand that for most people, deer season is a rite of passage in Michigan."

"No, Phillip, I understand, but...," Britt interrupted.

"Let me finish," Phillip continued. "Hunting is a proud tradition here. The first day of deer hunting is a school holiday, for goodness sake. You are fighting a losing battle."

Phillip turned back to Stephen. "Britt does not see how disliked she has become because of her opinions. She has become so unpopular we now have daily protestors who reside just outside my gate, as you observed when we drove in."

"So, that's who those people are." Stephen said.

"Yes, Stephen. And so far they have been very orderly and civil, but God knows, these people all own guns and I would not want them to trespass on my property. I've had to hire security now, just to make sure they don't get in."

Britt was about to respond but hesitated as Cora reappeared and set out a huge plate of turkey sandwiches. Cora placed a plate of steamed broccoli next to Britt and gave everyone their own bowl of salad. She returned from the kitchen and placed a plate of chocolate éclairs on the table for dessert.

Stephen noticed, once they all started eating, the conversation around the table subtly changed to an amenable buzz. It must have been the éclairs.

As everyone was finishing their desserts, Uncle Phillip stood up.

"Let's move to the trophy room. I have a little surprise."

Chapter 8

Phillip poured glasses of wine for all. He picked up a small rectangular package and handed it to Stephen.

"Stephen, I have a welcome gift for you. I hope you enjoy it."

Stephen was surprised and slightly embarrassed at all of the attention.

"You didn't have to do that, Uncle Phillip," Stephen said, as he struggled to tear wrapping paper off a decorative wooden box. Stephen opened the lid and saw a beautiful knife with a bone handle. Engraved on the handle was "Cliffside Manor, 1975". He picked it up and admired it.

"Thank you, Uncle Philip. It's beautiful."

"You're very welcome, Stephen. That knife was made in 1910 by the Marble Arms Company. The company is in Gladstone, the first city we passed outside of Escanaba.

"I remember when we went by there." Stephen said.

Uncle Phillip nodded.

"The Company is known worldwide for their excellent craftsmanship of hunting and outdoor accessories. Their older knives are eagerly sought after as collector's items. Don't lose your knife. Put it in a special place. I thought it would be fitting to give you a gift that was made here in Upper Peninsula."

Stephen balanced the knife in his hand. "It's a beauty, thanks again."

With Phillip, Britt and Jeanette all in the same room, the talk soon turned to business matters. Stephen wandered over to a shelf which held numerous plaques and awards for Uncle Phillip's films. He picked up a trophy for "Best Horror Script" for Attack of the Piltdown Man.

Stephen remembered in the movie the Piltdown man was something like a Neanderthal caveman brought back to life by a mad professor living in an isolated mansion deep in the moors of England. The movie had scared him when he watched it as a kid. Stephen set the trophy down and turned to his Uncle.

"Uncle Phillip, was there really a Piltdown man?"

"Yes and no," Uncle Phillip replied. "It was a famous hoax discovered as the archeological "missing link" in 1912. It turned out to be fabricated. Someone combined part of a human skull with an ape jaw. Can you believe it took over forty years to discover it was not real?"

"Who did it?" Stephen asked.

"Even now they don't know. Some think a man named Charles Dawson but other names are mentioned. Even Arthur Conan Doyle, the man who created Sherlock Holmes, has been mentioned."

"I've read some of his stuff," Stephen interrupted. "The Hound of the Baskervilles" is my favorite story."

"Well, Stephen, the Piltdown hoax proved to be a terrible embarrassment to many scientists, but it turned out to be the perfect story to base my movie on. It was a great mixture of some truth combined with a lot of fiction. Because of that movie, I'm considered to be the king of horror movies."

"Such a tribute," Britt laughed, tossed her hair back as she looked over at Stephen.

Phillip continued. "Speaking of movies, Britt, I'm putting together a meeting with some people to finance my next movie. I need to get back to Los Angeles in a few days to meet with them and I know they would be thrilled to meet you. Would you come with me this time?"

Britt moved close to Phillip, gave him a kiss on the cheek and started rubbing his arm.

"Honey, you know I hate to go back there. I hate the picture business and I hate leaving here even more. Go and have your meeting without me. I'm sure they will understand."

Phillip looked dejected.

"Think it over, Britt. You're turning into a recluse and you don't even see it."

Phillip was visibly upset. He put his drink down, turned around and marched out the door.

Chapter 9

Back in Grand View, Paulie glanced at his watch. It was three o'clock. He had driven up and down the few streets that made up the small town frantically searching for the Porsche that seemed to have disappeared in front of him. He pulled the car over and jumped out. He stretched, trying to get the kinks out of his broad shoulders and back. He was stuffed into a subcompact, the only car available to rent without a reservation. He felt like one of those big circus clowns driving around in a kiddy car.

Paulie noticed the building across the street contained a hardware store and a café. Just seeing the café sign reminded him he was hungry. He decided to take a break and get something to eat. Paulie walked across the street. As he was walking up to the restaurant, Paulie noticed a silver spotted skipper hovering above some flowers. He made a mental note to add some butterflies from this area to his collection.

As Paulie opened the door, he got the feeling that everyone in the restaurant had turned around to stare at him. He was still in the same rumpled suit he had put on in New York City. Everyone in the restaurant was either sporting a touristy shorts and sandal look, or was wearing what appeared to be the local fashion statement, a flannel shirt, jeans and work boots. Paulie sat down at a table for two. A waitress approached.

Without bothering to look at the menu, Paulie said, "Give me pastrami on rye with yellow mustard and a cup of black coffee."

"I'm sorry, Sir," the waitress replied. "We don't have any pastrami. Would you be interested in our luncheon special, the fresh lake perch plate?"

"No pastrami?" Paulie questioned. "What kinda deli is this?"

"This isn't a deli, Mister," the waitress replied, "It's the Grand View Café. Would you like a minute to take a look at our menu?"

Paulie grabbed the menu from the waitress's hand and slammed it open. Heads turned. His eyes ran down the menu…smelt, pasties, and rutabaga. What the hell is this? Paulie let out a sigh. This job was looking more discouraging as the day progressed. Already he had lost track of the damn kid, he was in a town of four hundred people, surrounded by woods in every direction, and now he was sitting in a restaurant where he had never even heard of half of the selections on the menu.

As the waitress walked to another table, Paulie shouted after her, "Just gimme a patty melt, fries and a cup of black coffee."

Waiting for his meal, Paulie glanced around the restaurant. The walls were knotty pine. Stuffed fish were displayed on every wall, each with a small price tag hanging from their tail. Through the large picture window in the front, he could see a huge expanse of water with an island about a half mile off shore.

Paulie wolfed down his lunch and got up to pay at the register. The same waitress took his money and rang him up. As Paulie grabbed his change, he had a thought.

"Who's the guy around here who drives that fancy silver Porsche?"

"You mean Mr. Kahle?"

Paulie leaned over the counter, "Yeah, that guy. Where could I find this Mr. Kahle?"

Immediately the waitress stiffened. "I'm not sure. I think he moved."

Paulie knew she was lying.

"Really, he moved did he?"

Paulie understood the waitress had spoken too quickly and from the look on her face, he knew she would not be providing him any more information. He walked out the door towards his car. Again, Paulie had a feeling that everyone was watching as he squeezed himself back into the tiny rental car. He looked back at the restaurant. Sure enough, several locals had walked over to the picture window and were staring at him. His first reaction was to flip them off, but he thought better of it. He started the car and headed out of town in the direction a billboard had indicated Cabins, one mile.

Paulie pulled up to a rustic motel and booked a room. The motel consisted of twelve small cabins set in a semi- circle connected by a common gravel driveway. He found his room, unpacked his suits and took a long hot shower. Paulie was standing in his underwear, drying off when he remembered to call and check in with Al.

"Hey Al, it's me, Paulie. I'm gonna give you my first report on the butterfly conspiracy."

"The what?"

"You know. I'm gonna tell you about that butterfly I'm after."

"Dammit, Paulie. Are you drunk?"

"No, Al. This is my code word. You know, like in them spy movies."

"Jesus, Paulie. Forget about the movies. Just tell me what the hell is going on, will you?"

"Okay. You ain't gonna believe this shit. I'm sitting in the middle of the woods about a thousand miles from nowhere. I'm so far out in the boonies, even the food these people eat is nothing I ever heard about. What do you say I just come back?"

"What about the kid?" Al asked.

"No problem. I been following him. He's with some rich guy named Kahle. What do you want me to do?"

There was a silence on the phone. Al said, "Listen, the kid's old man ain't paying up. You need to go to plan B and get the hell out of there. But don't screw up and don't let anyone see you. Got that?"

"Not a problem. Believe me Al, you've never seen nothing like this place, they don't even got a deli, can you believe that?"

Al replied, "Ain't that something. Look, Paulie, I gotta run."

Paulie slammed down the phone. Clearly Al didn't give a shit. Now that he got the go ahead, Paulie opened his "tool kit" to make sure everything was there: rope, blindfold, tape, and revolver.

Satisfied his supplies were ready, Paulie stretched out on the bed and soon fell asleep.

Chapter 10

Stephen and Jeanette were headed for a hike. They walked through the conservatory and stepped outside.

"Stephen, the trail I want to show you starts here. It winds around the big pond you can see from your window and then turns left and goes about half a mile along the cliff above Lake Superior. From there the trail goes straight, or you can take a short side trail to the right that leads to a spectacular overlook called The Log Slide."

"Why is it called The Log Slide?"

"Just what it sounds like. Loggers used to roll logs down this 300 foot sand dune into Lake Superior, where they would be rafted together and loaded onto lumber boats. The slope is so steep that sometimes the logs actually caught on fire from the friction."

"That must be some incline," Stephen marveled.

"It is. By the way, it's a great experience to slide down the huge sand dune. It only takes about twenty minutes to get to the bottom, but it takes a couple of hours to climb back up to the top. You should try it sometime."

"Sounds like fun. I'll try it."

"From the log slide trail, you can continue walking along the cliff, or you can take a shortcut, which leads to the back of Britt's cottage. The complete trail is a little over one mile, but it's less than half a mile if you take the shortcut."

Stephen gazed at the expanse of trees. "How much land does Uncle Phillip own?"

"He owns 120 acres with sixty acres along the Lake Superior shoreline. He bought at the right time. Now it would be impossible to buy that much property on Lake Superior."

She pointed to a break in the woods. "This trail continues past your uncle's property. His land backs up to the Pictured Rocks National Lakeshore. The lakeshore runs forty miles all the way to Munising."

As they continued along the walk, Stephen could not help but think how lucky he was to be escorted through this stunning scenery by such a pretty girl.

"Jeanette, you mentioned you're from this area, right?"

"Yes, my family's lived here for several generations. I'm half Indian and half French Canadian. I guess those trappers from long ago had more on their minds than animal skins," Jeanette said with a grin.

Your Uncle tells me you're going to study art in the fall."

"Yes, I'm very excited. I'm going to the Rhode Island School of Design. It's got a great reputation."

They spent an hour leisurely walking along the trail. Stephen noticed that the trail was starting to get a little damp and spongy.

"What's that?" Stephen asked, pointing to a huge mound rising from the middle of a large pond.

"It's a beaver dam. See the trees that have been chewed down all around here? Beavers used these trees to make the damn." Jeanette stopped to point. "Look, there's one swimming out in the water."

Stephen watched as the beaver maneuvered to a pile of sticks and tree limbs and disappeared.

"That's quite a complicated structure," he stated.

As they continued, the trail started climbing higher. At the top of a hill they intersected with a larger, more traveled path and Jeanette pointed to a sign.

"See Stephen, the path we were on isn't named because it's mostly on your uncle's private land. It intersects with this path, which is part of the Pictured Rocks Trail system. You should take some time and hike this section. It starts at Grand View and goes forty two miles along the lake to Munising."

"Forty two miles? I need to start getting in better shape. How long would it take to hike it?"

"A couple of days, but it depends on how much you wanted to walk each day. There are some interesting spots along the trail. One place is called Devil's Kitchen Cave. It's a cave where Indian legend has it that evil spirits roasted people."

"Now that's something I'd want to see!" Stephen said enthusiastically.

"I bet you do," Jeanette replied. "You can even see places where the cave is blackened with soot from fires. Kind of grisly if it's true. Personally, I think it's just a legend but if you stay on the trail you get to a beautiful rock formation called Miner's Castle."

"Would you hike it with me?" Stephen asked.

"I'd love to. We can do it in three or four stages."

The trail continued to climb. Finally, the trail broke out onto an overlook high above Lake Superior. Looking to the right, Stephen could see an island positioned just off the coast.

"I guess that's where Grand View gets its name," Stephen said.

"That's right, that's Grand Island."

To the left was a view of a pristine shoreline with an unbroken forest as far as the eye could see.

"This is spectacular!" Stephen exclaimed. "All this natural beauty and not a person in sight."

"Not exactly like New York City, is it?" Jeanette asked. "Hey, it's going to get dark soon. We better head back."

Jeanette led the way back down the trail. Stephen continued to admire the view, and it wasn't all trees that he was admiring. Halfway back, Jeanette said, "See that tree with the scratches on it?"

"Yes, what is it?"

"Bears. Bears mark trees like that for some reason. Maybe it's to mark their territory or just to sharpen their claws. You can see bear markings all through these woods."

They continued another ten minutes down the trail. After the bear comment, Stephen was looking behind every few minutes. After twenty minutes, Stephen stopped and said, "Let's take a break."

Jeanette pointed, "We can sit here."

They sat on a fallen log.

"Your uncle tells me you rode the train all the way from New York City. How long did that take?"

"Over 24 hours."

"Did you enjoy it?"

"Well, yes and no. I enjoyed seeing a lot of country, but, don't think I'm crazy, but I think someone may have been following me during my trip up here."

"What, someone followed you?"

"I know, it sounds nuts. I mentioned it to Uncle Phil, but I don't think he believed me."

"What makes you think someone followed you?"

Stephen related all his suspicions, from his traveling companion's fears, his Art Institute encounter, and the sighting in Escanaba.

"It does sound pretty coincidental, I must admit. Is there a reason someone would be following you? Are you running away from something that nobody knows about?"

"No, nothing like that. That's the problem. I can't think of any reason someone would be following me."

"Just like a mystery novel, eh? Or maybe you're a secret agent?" She smiled at him. Stephen colored slightly.

"Should I start calling you Bond? Secret agent Stephen Bond?"

He smiled back, embarrassed.

"Say, maybe we'd better get going before it gets too dark," Jeanette said, climbing to her feet.

Stephen jumped up and offered her a hand. They continued walking back toward the house.

Chapter 11

Paulie woke up and glanced at the clock radio sitting on the nightstand. It was seven thirty at night. He stretched, splashed some water on his face and opened the closet to get dressed. Damn suits, he muttered to himself. All the clothes he had taken were suits and it seemed like nobody around here was wearing anything but flannel shirts and jeans. He seemed to stick out like a sore thumb. He put on a dark blue suit, decided to forget about a tie and headed out the door.

While searching the town for the Porsche, Paulie had seen a bar on Lake Street. He decided to have a drink and maybe ask a few questions. Paulie kept his eye out for the Porsche on his drive back to town.

He opened the door to The Freighter View Tavern, headed straight towards the bar and ordered a whiskey and water. He looked around. The bar, just like the diner, seemed to have a combination of a few tourists and mostly locals. Paulie glanced at the guy sitting next to him. He was in his early twenties but didn't look very healthy. He was kind of thin and pale looking. He was drinking a bottle of beer. Paulie took a drink and turned to the man.

"How you doing?" Paulie offered.

"Just fine, I'm doing just fine," the man replied, a little hesitantly.

Trying to make conversation, Paulie gestured towards a photograph of a large boat on the wall.

"What kinda boat is that? I never seen a boat like that before."

"That's an ore boat. You'll see plenty of them around here. They haul iron ore from the mines up here to ports in Chicago, Minnesota and on into Canada."

"Iron? I wondered where that shit came from."

"I worked on the boats for a few years. You know, there's not a lot to do for work around here. I got hurt and had to quit."

The man stopped talking and took a sip of beer. He looked back at Paulie.

"What do you do? Sell insurance?"

Paulie paused. "Insurance? What the fu…," he stopped himself. "Ah, well, I guess you could say I'm in the insurance business," Paulie chuckled. "Let me get you a drink, Pal. What's your name?"

"They call me Moon. Moon Murchie." Moon didn't care for that last comment about insurance. It sounded a little sinister to him, but what the hell, a free drink was a free drink.

"And what's your name?" Moon inquired.

"Paulie."

With that said, Paulie turned and shot Moon a look Moon interpreted as meaning don't bother asking for my last name. Moon got the hint.

Moon Murchie hated his nickname. His real name was Francis, but around here, nicknames were easy to acquire and hard to shake.

Francis was thirteen years old when he got saddled with the name Moon. He was fishing with two other buddies along the shore of Grand Sable Lake when they saw a boat approaching. The boat was owned by one of their friends. As the boat got a little closer, the boys decided to have a little fun. Everyone turned around and, all together, they pulled down their pants.

Unfortunately for them, the boat had been borrowed by a sheriff's patrol out looking for a lost fisherman. The sheriff saw little humor in their prank and they all got arrested. Since Francis had previous run-ins with the law, the little prank ended his probation and he went downstate for a six-month stretch at a boy's reform school. The other kids got a reprimand and were sent home.

That incident earned him the nickname Moon. Once he got back, he couldn't lose the reform school past. It made locals wary of hiring him and Moon always seemed to be on the look out for an opportunity, as he was fond of saying.

Moon took a sip of his free beer.

Paulie asked, "Hey, Moonie. You live around here?"

"Yeah"

"What can you tell me about a guy named Kahle?"

"What's it too ya?"

Paulie stiffened. His first impression was to grab this little hick by the throat and ask him again. Paulie wasn't used to being asked questions. It was his job to ask the damn questions; but he did need some answers, so he took a moment to calm himself down and think of a reply.

"Ah…I'm up here looking at some property. You know, investment stuff, and his name keeps coming up. I know he drives a nice car and I think he may be just what I'm looking for as an investor, so to speak."

Moon took another sip of beer. "He's got dough, that's for sure. Have you ever seen his place, Cliffside Manor? He has to have a million bucks sunk into that place."

"No, I never been over there."

Paulie's heart was beating faster. "But I'd love to see it. Is it close?"

"Oh, yeah. About eight miles from here. Just when you come down the hill after the Grand View sign, you take a quick left on Pine Ridge Road and go back about two miles. There's a big gate, so you can't just drive in, but it's quite a site."

So that's how they disappeared so fast, Paulie thought. He finished his drink and ordered another round for himself and Moon.

"So what's there to do here at night? You got any clubs? You got an Italian Social Club, something like that?"

"Oh yeah, we got the Moose Lodge. On Fridays they cook up one hell of a fish fry. And the drinks are cheap, too."

"A lodge for moose," Paulie muttered, "now that's just goddamned perfect. All these damn trees and a lodge for Moose to go along with it. Just where the hell am I?"

"What?" Moon asked.

"Nothing, pal, nothing at all," Paulie said, shaking his head. "Nothing at all."

Chapter 12

Rain was pelting the window when Stephen woke up. He looked outside. Grey clouds were scurrying across the sky. It looked cold outside and his room felt damp. He had now been at Cliffside Manor for three days and this was the first bad weather he had encountered.

He showered, slipped on some warm clothes and headed downstairs for breakfast. The dining room was empty. Stephen glanced at his watch and was surprised to see that it was already nine-thirty. He had slept much longer than usual. It must have been the soothing sounds of the rain hitting against his window.

Uncle Phillip had mentioned that he would be working in his office most of the day and Stephen knew that meant Jeanette was probably busy too. Stephen had not figured out what Britt's schedule was. She came and went as she pleased, it seemed. Every time he saw her she always seemed to be dressed in something very flimsy and almost see through. With the weather outside being so cold and rainy, he wondered if she would be walking around in flannels today.

Stephen headed for the kitchen, which was located behind the dining room. As Stephen entered, Cora and a man were sitting at a table having coffee. At the sight of Stephen, Cora jumped up. "What can I get you for breakfast, Stephen?"

"Nothing, Cora. Sit down. I'll find something myself."

Cora poured Stephen a cup of coffee, handed it to him and walked back over to the table.

"I'd like you to meet Bobby Blankenship. Bobby's our security guard."

Bobby stood up to shake Stephen's hand. He was over six feet tall and had sandy blond hair. Stephen shook his hand.

"Nice to meet you. I've seen you walking outside, but we've never been introduced."

Bobby sat back down, and he and Cora returned to their conversation. Stephen dug through the cupboards and found a bagel and a blueberry muffin.

Stephen wandered over to the trophy room and sat in a huge brown leather chair, worn smooth from much use. A fire was burning. Stephen welcomed the warmth as he ate his bagel.

The night before, as he lay in bed, he kept thinking about the man who seemed to have been following him. Stephen felt a little embarrassed that he had mentioned his concern to two different people and it seemed neither of them had believed him.

With the bad weather, and both his uncle and Jeanette busy working, he thought it would be fun to check out the town of Grand View and possibly do some sketching. He could also ask a few questions, or maybe even find the guy who may have been following him. The guy certainly was big enough to spot!

Stephen heard a cough at the doorway. He turned around. It was Britt. No flannels for her. She was wearing a long sheer night gown, her hair was all tousled like she had just gotten out of bed. She was holding a cup of coffee.

"Morning, Stephen," she said as she approached him. "Did you sleep well?"

"Yes, very well." Stephen was about to ask, "and you?" but he thought better of it. He didn't want to have a vision of her in bed.

Britt pulled a cushion off the couch, tossed it on the floor and sat close to the fire. Stephen was uncomfortable. He wasn't sure it was a good idea to be alone in a room with such a sexy woman, especially with what she was wearing. Britt stared into the fire.

"With this weather, I doubt my fan club will be picketing the gate today. Such a relief. It makes your uncle so mad. I hate to cause trouble, but sometimes I just can't sit back and be silent."

Stephen didn't know what to say. To disagree with her would be rude, but to agree with her would be going against his uncle's wishes. He just silently sat there, feeling awkward. From the side, Stephen could see the full curve of her breast through the thin material of her negligee. The room he had thought felt chilly at first was now feeling much warmer.

"This cushion's hard," Britt said. As she stood up, Britt stepped on the hem of her night gown and fell over the arm of Stephen's chair, landing neatly in his lap. Stephen's coffee, which had been balancing on the arm of the chair, went crashing to the floor at the same time Uncle Phillip walked into the room.

"What broke?" Phillip asked.

Phillip's gaze moved from the shattered coffee cup on the floor up to the leather chair.

"Britt!"

Stephen jumped up from the chair so quickly Britt slid down to the floor. "Wait, Uncle, don't…"

Uncle Phillip stormed over to Britt. "Get out of here. Get back to the house."

He grabbed Britt's arm and walked her out of the room, shooting Stephen an icy stare.

Hearing the commotion, Jeanette appeared in the doorway. "What happened?" She asked. She took one look at Stephen and could tell whatever happened was not good.

"I was sitting in here by the fire finishing my breakfast when Britt skipped into the room wearing almost nothing. The next thing I know, she fell into the chair with me."

Stephen was watching Jeanette's face for a reaction. She didn't seem surprised or shocked at all.

He continued, "Before I could even move, Uncle Phillip came in and I think he jumped to a bad conclusion."

Stephen was visibly upset and he was speaking loudly. Jeanette bent down to pick up the pieces of Stephen's broken cup and saucer.

Bobby, the guard, appeared at the doorway.

"Everything okay?" he asked.

"Yes, Bobby." Jeanette said, "Everything's fine."

The guard turned and headed down the hallway behind Phillip and Britt.

"Stephen, settle down. I know this is putting you in a very uncomfortable position. Come with me, let's go upstairs where we can talk."

They marched up to the third floor without speaking. Jeanette pulled Stephen into the billiard room. A quiet tension filled the air.

"Do you play pool, Stephen?"

"A little. I never really played that much," Stephen said.

Jeanette grabbed two pool cues and handed one to Stephen. She racked up the billiard balls and said, "Go ahead, break."

Stephen hit the cue ball with a glancing blow. It hit the racked balls with only enough force to knock a few balls loose.

Jeanette took over and sunk five balls in a row. Stephen hesitated as he walked up to the table. His shot missed the ball completely. Jeanette grabbed the cues and set them back in the rack.

"Let's go to the library, I can see your heart's not in this game."

Once in the quiet surroundings of the library, Stephen regained his composure.

"I can't believe Uncle Phillip would think that I'd make a pass at his girlfriend? She's attractive, there's no discounting that. She's a lot older than me. How rude does he think I am?"

Stephen was pacing the floor. "I'm only here a few days and he thinks I'm making moves on his girlfriend. I've got enough women problems of my own now. I don't need any more."

Jeanette wondered what that statement meant but decided not to ask any questions.

"What's wrong with her, anyway, Jeanette? Parading around dressed like that in front of everybody."

"Stephen, I'm sure you were totally innocent and probably caught up in something with a little more history than you can even imagine."

Stephen stopped walking and sat on the arm of a chair, listening.

"Britt's a beautiful woman, but she is not as pretty as she once was. You remember your uncle pleading with her to go back to Hollywood with him?"

"Yeah, that kind of surprised me."

"Well, she loves it here with her animals and nature, she also shuns Hollywood."

"Why is that?" Stephen asked.

"Probably because she's not being offered the parts she once was. Britt got to where she was by being young and beautiful. She can see now there's another generation of young actresses who have taken her place."

"I never thought of that, it has to be hard."

"That's not easy for any woman, let alone one who has successfully used her looks and sensuality to achieve what she has become."

Stephen pondered Jeanette's words. "That makes sense, but why try and get me in trouble with my uncle?"

"Not to undermine your handsomeness," Jeanette said glancing down with a quick blush, "but I think this was more of a ploy for Britt to get your uncle jealous and have him pay more attention to her."

Stephen was trying to digest all of this.

"You were probably just a pawn. A handsome one, but a pawn, nonetheless."

Jeanette sighed, "I've worked here for years and, unfortunately, I've seen her in action before."

"I hope Uncle Phillip's not mad at me for long. I was going to get out of here for the day anyway. I was going to ask him to borrow a car and drive into Grand View."

"That's a good idea."

"I wanted to spend a little time looking for that goon that may have been following me, but I can't ask him for a car now. He's not even speaking to me!"

"Take mine. I think it would do you good to get out of here for a while and I'm supposed to be working. My car is just sitting there, so let's go back to my office and I'll get you the keys."

Stephen appreciated her support and he was thankful for the information she had shared with him. He had an urge to just grab her and give her a big hug, but he didn't want his uncle to pop in and get the wrong idea about that too!

Stephen controlled himself, thanked her for the use of her car, and slipped quietly out of Cliffside Manor, not wanting another confrontation.

An hour after Jeanette handed Stephen her car keys, Phillip appeared at her office door.

"Jeanette, have you seen Stephen?"

"About an hour ago. He wanted to drive over to Grand View so I let him borrow my car."

Phillip frowned. "What? Oh, that's not good. He should have stayed here."

"He was upset at what happened and felt terrible that you were mad at him. He felt a change of scenery would do him good."

"I was upset, but not at Stephen. I over reacted and I wanted to apologize. I guess I can do that later, but I wish he had not left the property."

"I thought it would be a good thing for him to get away, under the circumstances."

"Maybe not. Don't say anything to him, but I think it would be better for him to stay close to home for while."

Philip turned and headed back to the office.

Jeanette stood quietly. Was there more to Stephen's suspicion of being followed than it seemed?

Chapter 13

Stephen was surprised to find that Jeanette drove a Mustang convertible. The car was ten years old, but it seemed to be in excellent shape.

Stephen glanced up at the clouds. He spotted one small sliver of blue, enough reason to put the top down. Stephen folded the top down and turned on the heater.

As he waited for the gate to open, Stephen saw two young men and a girl jump up and grab signs. They waved their signs at his passing car. Stephen could read two of the signs; "Don't Mess With Our Hunting Rights" and "Venison, it's OUR dinner!". The guy with the third sign was waving it too fast for Stephen to read as he drove by. They seemed harmless enough.

It only took about ten minutes to get into town. After driving around, it appeared to Stephen that Grand View consisted of about 10 streets with a few motels, three restaurants, a bar, two gas stations and a small IGA grocery store.

In a very short time, Stephen had driven up and down each street several times. There was no sign of the man Stephen thought may have been following him. Stephen pondered what to do next. The only place that seemed to have any visible activity was a bar called The Freighter View. He thought it wouldn't hurt to stop in and see if he could learn anything there.

Stephen entered and took a seat at the bar. He was just about to order a soda when the bartender slammed a foamy draft beer down in front of him and gestured over to two young men sitting to his right.

"It's from Scott", the bartender said.

Surprised, Stephen took a sip, turned and said, "Thanks, but isn't it a little early for a beer?"

Scott and his buddy sauntered over. "Yeah, it's early. We just got rained out and there's nothing much to do so we come over here. I made a bet with my cousin Joe, here, and I lost. The bet was I had to buy the first person who comes into the bar a beer. You were that guy."

"Guess it is my lucky day." Stephen laughed. "What was the bet?"

"See that dog sitting over there? Joe here thought Frankie, the new bartender, would kick us out when we come in here with my dog. Turns out the guy loves dogs, so no problem."

Stephen looked over and saw an animal that appeared to be a lot closer to a wolf than a dog.

"That's a dog?" Stephen asked.

"You betcha. Well, kind of. He's a Czechoslovakian wolf dog."

"I've never heard of that," Stephen said.

"It's a cross between a German shepherd and a timber wolf. We call him King. A guy give him to me cause he was afraid of him. Now that's not good. You can't show any fear around this dog. You gotta be the boss. I handled German Shepherd's when I was over in 'Nam so the guy knew I could handle this one."

Stephen marveled at the dog's resemblance to the wolf he had seen on the way to Grand View.

"Does he make a good pet?"

Scott laughed. "No, sir. He's a one man dog but not much of a pet. I would never bring him in here if it was crowded. But this early, I knew the Freighter would be almost empty. Most people take a look at him and stay away."

"I can understand that. Looks like something you wouldn't want to mess with. By the way, Scott, I'm Stephen."

Scott was curious because Stephen didn't have the typical tourist look. He didn't have the typical camper or backpacker look, either.

"So Stephen, are you checking out the sites or staying with someone in town?"

Stephen explained that he was staying at his Uncle Phillip's place for the summer.

"Oh, that's a good one," Scott laughed. "Joe, did you hear that? This guy's parked at the fancy Kahle place and I'm buying him a beer?"

Scott smacked the bar with his hand, "Now ain't that something. But you know what? Your uncle's done a bunch of good things for this area, so damnit, I'm happy to get you a beer."

"What about you guys?" Stephen asked. "Do you live around here?"

"Yeah, my folks have a campground just out of town," Scott said. "Joe and I work there. We're putting up a rec center right now. The rain put us out of business, at least for now."

Stephen bought beers for Scott and Joe.

"I need to ask you guys a question. Have you seen a big guy with a dark complexion, nose looks like it was broken a time or two? He usually dresses in a suit. He looks like this." Stephen pulled out a sketch he had ripped out of his sketch pad.

Both Scott and Joe started laughing. Joe said, "Scotty, that's the big guy we saw talking with Moon last night, right here."

Scott studied the picture.

"Yeah, that's the guy. Holy wah, anyone who would be drinking with Moon has to be from out of town!" Scott laughed. "Is this guy a friend of yours?"

"Not quite. I have a pretty strong suspicion he followed me here from New York City, but I'm not sure. I need to find out what he's doing here and see if any of his plans involve me."

"Well, that's easy," Scott said. "Joe, give Moon a call. Tell him we're sitting down at the Freighter. Tell him we want to buy him a pitcher of beer."

Scott grinned at Stephen. "Believe me, that'll get him down here."

The front door of the freighter swung open and two girls walked in.

"Scotty, them two are the babes that are staying in the tent on lot 18," Joe said. "Remember how cute I told you they were."

Scott turned to see. "They're all cute to you, Joe."

Joe ignored Scott's remark. "I'm gonna walk over and talk to them after I give Moonie a call," Joe said, climbing off the bar stool.

"Like, I'm surprised," Scott responded.

Twenty minutes later Moon walked in and sat down next to Scott. Stephen ordered Moon a pitcher of beer.

"What's going on? Why in hell's name are you guy's buying me free beer? I dragged my ass down as fast as I could. This better not be your idea of some kind of prank, eh."

"Calm down, Moonie. We think you may know something that could help out our friend Stephen over here."

Stephen reached over and shook Moon's hand. "Nice to meet you."

"Remember that big, ugly guy in the suit you was yapping to last night?" Scott asked.

"Yea, you mean the guy from New York?"

"I guess. We just need to know the guy's story, that's all. Now, that's worth a free pitcher, right?"

"And just why is that any of his business?" Moon asked, looking over at Stephen.

"Cause it is," Scott replied. "You want that free pitcher or not?"

"I suppose. I didn't come down here just to stare at you."

Moon poured a glass of beer, took a long swig and said, "Like I said, he ain't from around here. I don't know much, just that he was looking for some business partners who had a bunch of dough and he wanted to know where Mr. Kahle lived. So I told him. He showed up at the picket line this morning, nosing around."

Scott watched as the color seemed to drain from Stephen's face.

Chapter 14

Phillip was in the library working on the latest revisions to the script for his next movie. His last few movies had not done as well as expected. He knew it would be very difficult, if not impossible, to duplicate the success of his most lucrative films. The popularity of the B-movie horror genre he had single-handedly revived was waning. The new trend was slasher movies, full of explicit blood and gore. This was a direction he would not allow himself to go, no matter how financially successful it appeared to be.

Phillip caught himself reading the same page three times. Clearly he was not concentrating. He wondered if Stephen had returned. He looked out the window to where Jeanette usually parked her car. The spot was empty. Phillip wished Stephen had not ventured into town alone. He walked down to Jeanette's office and asked if she had seen Stephen return. She had not.

Phillip walked outside. The guard was walking back from checking on the protestors at the gate.

"Bobby", Phillip called. "Have you seen Britt?"

"I think she's back at the cottage, Mr. Kahle. I saw her go in the back after her walk this morning."

Phillip walked along the path that skirted the edge of the pond and ended at the back of Britt's house next to the mansion. Phillip used his key and entered. He could hear muted sounds from a television coming from the living room. Britt was lying on the couch watching a black and white movie. She glanced over when he entered the room.

"Once again, your antics have caused trouble," Uncle Phillip said, staring at Britt.

"Not this lecture again."

"I would hardly call a discussion about you trying to seduce my nephew a lecture."

Britt sighed. "Darling, it was just an accident. I tripped on my gown."

"That flimsy thing isn't something you should be walking around in anyway. Especially when I have company."

"I know, maybe you're right. I walked in to have my coffee in the trophy room and your nephew's eyes almost popped out of his head."

Phillip glared at her.

Britt continued, "Didn't you say his parents had cooped him up in a stuffy prep school for the last six years? You can tell he doesn't feel comfortable around women."

She stood up and wrapped her arms around Phillip. She kissed him hard on the lips.

"Come upstairs, darling. You know you're the only man I love."

Chapter 15

It was apparent to Scott that the information Moon provided did not set well with their new friend. Scott walked over to the table where Joe was sitting with the girls.

"Come on Joe, lets get out of here."

"Are you kidding me?" Joe slowly rose from the chair.

"We gotta leave now?" He looked back at the table.

"Yeah, let's go," Scott said. "Come with us, Stephen. We want to take you for a ride."

Joe and Stephen got into Scott's car. King jumped in the back seat with Joe. Stephen said it seemed a little awkward to leave Moon just sitting there by himself. Both Joe and Scott agreed that Moon would be fine as long as he had his free beer.

"Forget about Moon," Joe piped in. "Here I am, making time with the two prettiest girls we've seen all summer and now I gotta leave."

"Come on, Joe. You gab to every girl that walks into the freighter. I never seen anything like it."

Joe laughed.

"I wanted to show Stephen our place, here," Scott continued.

After a few minutes Scott turned the car into the entrance of the Grand View Campgrounds. They all piled out and Scott took Stephen for a tour. Scott pointed out the twenty two campsites, the soon to be completed recreation hall and the stream that meandered along the back of the property.

"There's great fishing in that little stream," Joe proudly declared.

They followed Scott to a picnic table and sat down.

"Stephen," Scott said, "I started thinking about a few things when Moon was telling us about that guy. You didn't look so happy when Moonie said the big guy was asking questions and went over to your uncle's place."

Scott turned to Joe. "Remember Aunt Rose telling us about that rude guy she waited on at the diner?"

"Yeah, the big guy that could hardly fit into his car?" Joe asked.

"I think that's the same guy that's been asking questions about Mr. Kahle."

"He sounds like a jerk to me," Joe said.

"Stephen, your uncle has really helped out around here," Scott said. "He started a scholarship fund and he gave money to rebuild the Moose Hall a few years back."

"Some people are jealous of what he has," Joe interrupted. "And I know a couple of guys who aren't too crazy about his girlfriend. Her views on hunting, most of all."

Scott looked at Stephen. "That's true. But I think most of us around here are damn happy with what Stephen's uncle has done. We know who belongs here and who doesn't and it looks like this guy from New York is looking to start some trouble."

Stephen said, "I'm kind of worried because I don't have a clue of why this guy would be following me. He has to be up to something."

Scott laughed. "If he's the same guy my Aunt Rose ran into, I think you're right. Maybe we can make this guy want to get the hell out of here and go back to wherever he came from."

"I appreciate your help, I really do," Stephen said. "Count me in, I want to help out if I can. Don't forget, it's my problem, not yours."

Scott just grinned, "We have to find the guy first."

Stephen glanced at his watch. "This has been great. Thanks for showing me around the campground. I need to get going, there's a situation I want to take care of back at my uncle's place."

Scott and Joe dropped Stephen off at Jeanette's car. As Stephen drove off, they walked back into the bar.

Scott ordered two beers and asked, "Joe, do you remember what happened when we went camping with our scout troop in the seventh grade."

"You mean that trick my dad's friend, Mr. Miller, played on us out in the woods?"

"Yeah."

"What about it? Oh, wait a minute. Are you thinking what I'm thinking?"

Scott started to laugh.

"Scotty, remember how mad my dad got at Mr. Miller because of that?"

"Yeah, I remember. Big deal. It all blew over pretty quick."

"You think so? I don't think Freddie DeGrand has ever spoken to him since then, and that happened over 7 years ago."

"Joe, if we needed to get down to the basement of the lodge, does your old man still have a key?"

"Sure. He cleans up the place every Sunday morning, just like always."

"Great, I want you to go get something for us and put it in your car so it's ready if we ever need it."

"Oh, boy," Joe said, shaking his head. "Here we go again."

Stephen had mixed emotions about his first trip to Grand View. He had made friends with two great guys, but he also confirmed for sure that somebody was actually following him. Every few minutes on the way back to Uncle Phillip's Stephen checked the rear view mirror to make sure there wasn't a suspicious car tailing him.

Uncle Phillip was waiting in the trophy room when he returned. Phillip was feeling much better about the whole situation after seeing Britt.

"Stephen, can we talk?"

"Sure."

Uncle Phillip asked how his trip to Grand View had gone. Stephen mentioned that he had enjoyed the trip, had met two new friends and had been given a tour of the Grand View Campground. He didn't mention anything about the other information he had learned.

Phillip knew about the campground and told Stephen he knew Scott's parents, but he couldn't place Joe.

Phillip put his arm around Stephen, "I want to apologize for my behavior this morning. That was not so good. Britt, she's very good at irritating me. I'm sorry you were dragged into this. Will you accept my apology?"

"Certainly, Uncle Phil. I'm just relieved you understand I didn't have anything to do with what happened this morning."

"No, no, I understand completely," Phillip stated. "This won't happen again, believe me."

Uncle Phillip turned to leave. "I'm glad we had this talk. I'm working on something in the library. By the way, it was nice of Jeanette to let you use her car, but I have a car set aside for you to use whenever you wish. Find Bobby, he'll show you where it is."

"Okay, thank you."

"Oh, Cora needed to go to Munising today so we're just grabbing something to eat out of the kitchen. She left us a plate of fried chicken and there's some home-made soup in the crock pot. Help yourself whenever you're hungry. She'll be back later to prepare supper."

Stephen had not felt hungry until Uncle Phillip mentioned food. Stephen made his way back to the kitchen.

As he entered, once again the guard was sitting at the table. Apparently, the kitchen doubled as the guard office. This time Bobby was sitting alone.

Stephen poured himself a cup of coffee, grabbed a chicken leg, a steaming cup of soup and sat down at the kitchen table with Bobby.

"Anything interesting in the paper?" Stephen asked, trying to make conversation.

The guard glanced up.

"Not really," Bobby replied returning his gaze back to his paper. Stephen took a bite of chicken. The silence felt awkward.

"How long have you worked here?" Stephen asked.

"Three years," Bobby responded, not looking up.

Stephen gave up trying to be polite. He grabbed a part of the paper Bobby appeared to have finished reading and continued eating his lunch. He wondered why the guard was being so unfriendly. He hoped it wasn't because he viewed Stephen as family. That would just be stupid.

Stephen finished his lunch and stood up. "My uncle said you would show me the car he has ready for me. Can we do that now?"

Bobby tossed down his paper. "It's in the garage."

The garage was set back and to the left of Britt's cottage. They walked in silence. Stephen was amazed when he saw six shiny vehicles parked in the garage. Bobby pointed out a fully restored red 1960 MG.

"That's the car Mr. Kahle would like you to use."

Stephen walked up to the car. "It's beautiful! How long has he had it?"

Stephen waited a few seconds for an answer. He turned towards Bobby only to see him headed back to the main house. Stephen wondered what the problem was with him. He opened the driver's side door of the MG and peered inside. The car looked like it was brand new.

Stephen spent the rest of the afternoon sitting in the conservatory, reading a book from the library. After supper, Uncle Phil suggested they all retreat to the trophy room.

Phillip pulled out a card game called 'Michigan Rummy' and insisted they all play. Stephen resisted at first, because he had not played many card games, but the game was easy to learn. They spent the next three hours playing cards, drinking and having many laughs.

Uncle Philip looked at his watch. "My goodness, it's almost eleven o'clock. I think we've played enough cards for one night."

He folded up the Michigan Rummy board, said good night to everyone and got up to leave. As he was leaving, Britt also said her good nights and walked out, arm-in-arm with Phillip.

Stephen walked with Jeanette as far as her door and then headed up to his room. Once in his room, he pulled out his sketch book, some charcoal sticks and started sketching. He was feeling very content. His uncle's place was far removed from New York City. He had met some very interesting people and he was sure this was going to be a summer to remember. He hadn't thought of Jill for quite some time.

He walked over to the window. The wind had picked up and he could hear it whistling through the pines. Stephen watched as whitecaps rose down along the shoreline. He returned to his chair and picked up his sketch book.

His door was only partially closed. He heard soft footsteps outside in the hall. He glanced up from his sketch and saw Britt, holding a book, as she walked past his door. She was wearing a silky floor length robe that covered her feet. She moved so quietly and smoothly it appeared that she was gliding along the floor.

Stephen turned back to his drawing. He was trying to sketch an Indian standing on a cliff looking towards Lake Superior, but it just wasn't working out the way he had intended. He remembered seeing a book of American Indians sitting open on a table in the library. That book would be perfect source material for his sketch.

He started for the library then stopped. Maybe it was not such a good idea being in the library alone with Britt, after what had happened. After a moment of speculation, he decided that he wasn't going to hide from Britt for the whole summer. He would just go straight to the library, grab the book and head back to his room.

Stephen approached the open library door. He stepped in and looked around. No Britt. He walked over and picked up the book. It was on the oak table just where he remembered it. He glanced around the library again. Britt was nowhere to be seen.

Stephen returned to his room. He found a picture of an old Indian chief with a very weathered and sculptured face. It was perfect. He started sketching. He wondered how Britt could have left the library and gone back downstairs without him noticing. Stephen thumbed through the book and started reading about the various Indian tribes that had inhabited northern Michigan. He set his sketchbook aside and took the book over to the bed.

After twenty minutes, he fell asleep, the book resting heavily on his chest.

Chapter 16

The next day, Stephen was restless. Uncle Phillip was busy working and Stephen could see Jeanette going back and forth from her office to Uncle Phillip's.

He walked up to the library, but once there, the sunshine and clear blue sky made it impossible for Stephen to want to stay inside. He decided to take a walk. Stephen headed downstairs and made his way to the conservatory. The room was huge with floor to ceiling windows running along each wall. Potted plants were arranged around the perimeter of the room and brown rattan furniture with green cushions was set in assorted groupings.

Stephen walked outside. Immediately, the warmth of the sun beat down on him. It seemed the Manor always had a slightly damp feeling inside, no matter what the weather was like. When Jeanette had shown him this path the first time, they had walked to the right. Seeking a different view, Stephen turned left. The path meandered between the conservatory and the pond. Many different kinds of flowers were planted and the shrubs were well manicured. Once Stephen reached the end of the main house, the path continued over to Britt's cottage.

"Hello, Stephen."

Stephen turned to see Britt sitting on a bench under a vine covered trellis. She was drinking coffee and smoking a cigarette while flipping through a magazine. To Stephen, Britt reminded him of a picture of Jayne Mansfield he had seen in a purloined men's magazine back at school. Her breasts looked like ice cream cones under her soft, short sleeved, angora sweater.

Britt motioned for Stephen to join her.

"Cigarette?" Britt offered.

"No, thanks."

"So, how are you enjoying your summer at Cliffside Manor?" Britt asked.

"It's great. The estate is spectacular and everyone's been so friendly. I'm looking forward to doing some hiking along the lake. I really needed to get away."

"I know. I love it here. It's so quiet and out of the way. I feel peaceful being surrounded by these forests."

Britt paused to take a puff from her cigarette.

"Your uncle is always trying to get me to go with him back to Hollywood, but the thought of leaving, even for a short time, is unbearable."

"I've never been to California, but I've always heard it was nice."

"I don't have many good memories of my time in California. It can be a very nasty place, professionally speaking. Enough about that."

Britt shook her head. "Phillip tells me that you were supposed to be backpacking in Europe but those plans fell through."

"Talk about unpleasant memories. Yes, my supposed girlfriend bailed out on me at the last minute and told me she was going to Europe with another guy. I just didn't see that coming."

Britt turned to Stephen and put her hands on his arm. "You're a very handsome man, Stephen. I'm sure there are many other beautiful girls just waiting for you to ask them out."

One of Britt's hands was rubbing his arm while the other was caressing the top of his hand. Stephen was feeling very uncomfortable. The last thing he needed was to have Uncle Phillip walk around the corner and see this.

Stephen stood up. "Thanks for the kind words, Britt. I hope you're right." He pulled his hand away.

"I'm going to continue my walk and enjoy this morning breeze before it goes away. I'll see you back at the house."

Britt did not reply. She glanced down and returned to her magazine.

Stephen headed down the trail that led to the log slide overlook. He walked over to the small retainer wall and stared out over the lake. He watched as two hikers walked along a trail. The cliff was so high, they looked to be only about an inch tall.

Stephen's encounter with Britt made him think about Jill again. He wondered where she was in Europe and what she was doing. He wondered if she ever thought about him anymore.

Suddenly Stephen felt a force push hard against his shoulders. Before he could steady himself, he went sailing over the wall. He fell straight down ten feet, hit the soft sand of the dune and started to tumble uncontrollably down the steep slope. He tried desperately to stop rolling and slow his decent.

After falling halfway down the three hundred foot incline, Stephen was able to turn onto his back and slide the rest of the way feet first. Sand was hitting him everywhere. It was in his hair, his mouth and under his shirt.

Finally, he stopped sliding. Stephen lay still at the edge of the shore. He was winded and shaken up. Thankfully, the soft sand had prevented any broken bones.

Stephen stood up and shook the sand from his body. He looked back up to the distant cliff edge. He didn't see anyone, but that did not surprise him. He continued to brush the sand out of his hair and started the long climb back up to the overlook.

Lunch was over by the time Stephen scaled the dune. It didn't make a difference, he was too exhausted to eat. He went up to his room, took a shower and flopped onto his bed.

Stephen was awakened by a soft knock. His muscles ached as he got up and headed for the door.

"Hi, Jeanette. Come in."

"Are you okay?" She asked him.

"Yeah, why do you ask?"

"Everyone was a little worried. You didn't show up for lunch and nobody has seen you all afternoon. Britt said she saw you this morning headed to the overlook, but nobody's seen you since. I thought I would check to see if you were in your room."

"I'm fine, I guess. Remember how you said I should slide down the log slide and then climb back up someday?"

"Yes."

"Well guess what? That's what I did today."

"Oh, it sure didn't take you long to give it a try. You must be very adventurous."

"Not as adventurous as you may think. It wasn't even my idea."

"What do you mean?"

"I was pushed!"

Jeanette looked puzzled. "Pushed? Who pushed you?"

"Good question. I don't know."

Chapter 17

The next day, as they worked at the campground, Scott and Joe fine-tuned their plan of what to do if they were lucky enough to run into the guy Stephen thought was following him.

"Scotty," Joe said. "This reminds me of those mystery books we used to read as a kid."

"I know. You're already Joe, so maybe you should be calling me Frank from now on," Scott said with a laugh.

After supper, they headed straight over to The Freighter to see if their suspect showed up. They had toyed with the idea of calling Moon to come too, but decided they didn't need him. Scott thought they could recognize the guy if he came in, based on Stephen's sketch.

In the car, Scott asked Joe, "Are we all set?"

"Yeah, it's in the trunk. Let's hope the guy shows."

"If he's gonna go out, where else can he go?" Scott asked.

As they approached the bar, Scott and Joe peered into the big plate glass windows. A few tourists were sitting at tables, but no sign of the guy and no sign of Moon, either. They took their usual places at the bar.

"Where do you think Moon is? I thought he about lived in this place," Joe asked.

"I heard he was getting some dough to hold a sign in front of Mr. Kahle's place."

"No shit!" Joe exclaimed. "Who's footing the bill for something as stupid as that?"

"I heard it was some big national hunting organization. I guess they're fed up with the stink Mr. Kahle's girlfriend is causing. She was on the news a few months ago, remember?"

"I wonder if this guy we're looking for has anything to do with that?" Joe asked.

"Hmmm, I wond..." Scott's sentence was cut off. Scott was looking into the large mirror behind the bar.

"Joe, look who's coming in."

Joe glanced up at the mirror. Sure enough, a man fitting Stephen's description was opening the door. Crumpled suit, dark complexion, nose on the side of his face. He walked straight towards them and sat down two barstools to Joe's right.

"Bingo!" Joe whispered.

Paulie ordered a whiskey and water and looked around. The place was pretty empty. The two guys next to him looked to be locals, everyone else seemed to be tourists. Paulie still needed a little more information.

Paulie motioned to the bartender, "Hey buddy, get these two guys a beer on me."

The bartender set down two drafts in front of Scott and Joe and nodded, indicating that they had come from the man in the suit.

Scott jumped to the occasion. He drained what was left of his first beer, grabbed the one Paulie had just bought and headed over to where he was sitting.

"Thanks for the beer."

Scott held out his hand. "I'm Scott and this is my cousin Joe."

"You guys from around here?" Paulie asked, even though he thought he knew the answer.

Joe piped in, "Yeah. We work at the Grand View Campground. Real nice place. You should check it out if you need a place to stay."

"A campground? No, not for me. I got a nice room at the Log Slide Mot…," Paulie stopped short. "Ah, I'm staying in a place down the road."

Scott took a sip from his beer. "If you got some free time, there's a lot of things to see around here. We got the Pictured Rocks, that's nice. Have you been to Tahquamenon Falls? It's about a hundred miles from here, but it's real nice, too."

"No. I got some business up here," Paulie said. Scott pretended not to hear him. Scott gave a nod to Joe.

"Another interesting place is that big house just outside of town," Joe said. "You can't go in and walk around, but it's kind of famous around here. It belongs to a movie director named Kahle. You ever heard of him?"

Paulie gave a start. "Yeah, I heard of him."

"That guy's a piece of work," Joe continued. "He drives around in a fancy car like he owns the place. He gets people to work for him and he don't pay them shit. We can't stand the pompous ass."

Paulie perked up. "Really? I got this guy that wants me to take a look at that place, but I hear you can't get past the gate. I drove over there yesterday. There was a bunch of guys walking around with some signs. I didn't know what they were up to so I got the hell outta there."

"Why does he want you to take a look at the place?" Scott asked.

"It's one of them real estate deals. My guy's real famous. He don't want everyone to know he's looking to buy. You know, then the damn price goes up."

"I didn't know Cliffside Manor was for sale?" Joe asked.

"Good," Paulie said. "That's the way my guy wants it, you know what I mean?"

"I guess so," Joe replied.

"So, you guys know a way to get in there other than through that damned locked gate, so I can take a good look around?"

"Are you kidding me?" Scott said. "That's easy. I know an old logging road that can get you right to the back of that property."

Paulie reached into his back pocket and pulled out his wallet. He flashed a twenty dollar bill and said, "How about you show me and then we all forget anything happened?"

"You've got a deal," Scott said, "but keep your money. If we're lucky, your buddy will buy Kahle's place and the asshole will move back to Hollywood where he belongs. You want to go now before it gets real dark?"

"Yeah, let's go!" Paulie nodded.

Scott, Joe and Paulie all piled into Scott's car. As they drove out of town, Scott told Paulie about the old logging road they were headed to and how it meandered through the woods, finally ending up very close to the back of Cliffside Manor. Most of Scott's information was true except the logging road ended up going miles in the opposite direction of Mr. Kahle's property. Scott was not worried about this slight inaccuracy. If their plan worked, old Paulie would not be getting anywhere near Cliffside Manor.

The car turned onto the opening of a narrow, bumpy road. It had been a logging road forty years ago when loggers were working the land. Now, it was just a narrow overgrown path through dense forest.

Scott drove about a quarter of a mile and pulled over into a small clearing. They all got out. Paulie looked around. It was much darker in the forest than it had been on the main road.

Joe said, "Yous guys get started. I've got to take a leak. Too many beers, I'll catch up."

"Okay", Scott said. "Come on, Paulie, it's this way."

They started walking down the dense path. Paulie was moving slowly, his head turning from side to side. Scott was ahead of him, walking faster. Scott turned around to see where Paulie was.

"Come on, we need to get there before it gets dark."

Paulie started running up to Scott. "Hey, not do damn fast. This ain't a walk in the park. Maybe it's too dark for this tonight. I'm thinking tomorrow is probably a better deal. You know, with more light and everything."

Scott just kept walking.

Joe watched as they disappeared around the first turn in the path. He quietly popped opened the trunk and unrolled a bear skin rug that normally covered the floor in the basement of the Moose Lodge. He draped it over his shoulders and headed to a shortcut through the woods.

Every time Paulie heard a sound in the forest he would slow down and peer into the dense underbrush. This was causing Scott to get further and further ahead. Paulie looked up just in time to see Scott disappear around a bend in the path, two city blocks ahead.

"You son-of-a-bitch, wait for me!" he yelled.

Paulie's heart was pounding. He was alone on the path, deep in the darkening woods. Paulie walked faster, hoping to catch up with Scott. The bushes exploded with a big crash right next to him. What the hell was that!

He froze in fear as a black bear rose up less than six feet away. It growled and lunged at him.

Paulie screamed. He dove off the path and started running blindly through the woods. Tree limbs slapped against his face and he stumbled to his knees. He got up and kept running. A sharp branch caught his suit coat. Paulie felt a tug and heard a ripping sound. He didn't slow down.

Finally, winded, Paulie came to a stop. He bent over and heaved to catch his breath. He listened. The woods were quiet. The only sound Paulie could hear was his heavy breathing and the sound of his heart pounding. He was lost in the middle of the forest and it was almost dark.

He glanced around. There was no path, just an endless maze of trees. He wondered if it was safe to call out for Scott and Joe or would that just lead the bear right to him? Poor Joe, he was probably being ripped apart by the bear right now.

Paulie sat down on a stump and started to shake. His legs felt damp. He looked down and muttered, "Shit, I've pissed my pants."

Joe did all he could to not laugh out loud. He rolled up the bear skin rug and headed back to the car. Scott was already behind the driver's seat. Joe jumped in and they drove off. They were laughing too hard to even talk during the ride back to the bar. They parked in front of the Freighter View. Scott held the door open for Joe.

"What a great job, Joe. After that in-your-face bear meeting, I hope Mr. New York tough guy packs up and heads back to the city. Let's get Stephen down here so he can laugh his ass off."

Stephen was surprised to get Scott's call. He could tell from Scott's voice that something was up, but Scott wasn't talking.

"Sure, I'll meet you at the Freighter. Give me a few minutes, I'll see you then," Stephen said.

He walked down to the garage and picked up the car Bobby had pointed out for him to use.

As he was leaving the estate, Stephen drove by several protestors at the gate, before heading down Route 77. The top was down and a cool wind was blowing through his hair. Scott had been laughing so hard on the phone Stephen had no idea what he was talking about, other than a request to meet him and Joe at the Freighter View.

When Stephen entered the bar, Scott and Joe were still going strong. So strong, in fact, they didn't even see him enter.

Joe was crouched over with his arms outstretched yelling, "Grrrrrr, Grrrrrr, Grrrrr'.

Scott was doubled up, holding his sides from laughing. Stephen approached the two.

"What's going on?"

Scott took a moment to recover.

"When you left the campground, me and Joe came up with a plan to play a trick on that big oaf that's been following you and asking a bunch of questions about your uncle."

Well, we really didn't think of it," Joe interrupted. "It was a trick that got played on us when we were kids. Scared the shit out of us, too."

Scott continued, "It did. So we figured maybe we could repeat the pleasure if we ever ran into your friend from New York City."

"And we did," Joe said, with a huge grin.

"So what did you do?" Stephen asked.

"Well, we decided to come down to the Freighter tonight to see if he showed up," Scott said.

"Not really going out of our way too much," Joe added, "since we're down here about every night, anyway."

Scott waved for him to shut up. "So anyway, from the picture you showed us, we knew him the minute he walked in. He sat right next us and the asshole even bought us a beer. Then he starts asking questions about how he wants to check out your uncle's place, but he don't want anyone to know."

"Did he say what he was looking for?" Stephen asked Scott.

"He said some guy wanted to buy the place, but we knew that was bullshit. We told him we knew an old logging road that would take him to the back of the place."

Joe saw the worried look on Stephen's face. "Don't worry, Stephen," Joe interrupted, "it doesn't go anywhere near your Uncle's place."

Scott continued, "When we stopped the car and got out, Joe stayed back and I started walking him down a path in the woods. His name is Paulie, in case you didn't know. So Paulie and I started walking down the road. It was getting dark and I started walking faster and faster."

Joe piped in, "I stayed back, told him I had to pee, so I could put on a bearskin rug my old man let me take from the Moose Lodge. I snuck around and came crashing out of the woods right next to him."

Joe started laughing again. "He screamed like a little baby and ran like hell into the woods."

"So what happened to him? Where is he?" Stephen asked.

"Who knows? Still crashing around out there, I guess," Joe laughed.

Scott and Stephen joined in.

Chapter 18

Paulie sat frozen on a stump, afraid to move or make a sound. It was getting darker, and colder. After about half an hour, Paulie noticed a yellow glow appear through the trees. The moon was rising. It was only a quarter moon, but it provided enough illumination to penetrate the blackness of the woods.

As the moon slowly rose above the trees, Paulie could see the ridge of a cabin roof looming only a few hundred feet in front of him. His spirits lifted. A cabin meant safety. Even if it was locked, Paulie knew he could break in. Paulie started walking through the woods towards the structure.

He stopped as he approached a clearing surrounding the cabin. He listened. There was no sound and the cabin was dark.

Paulie took a tentative step out into the clearing. He stopped. Again, no sign that anyone was around. He walked over to the front porch. Old timbers creaked as he mounted the steps. He leaned over to a window and peered into the darkness. He tried the door. Locked.

He walked around to the back, stopping at another window. He tried to open it. It didn't budge. He approached the back door and wasn't surprised to find it locked, as well.

Paulie picked up a stick and smashed out the bottom pane of glass in the door. He stopped to listen. Nothing stirred in the cabin. Paulie reached inside, twisted the knob and walked inside.

The cabin was small. There was just an open kitchen to the living room area with one small bedroom. A cast iron stove was sitting in the living room. There was no bathroom, but an outhouse could be seen out back. Two bunk beds were in the tiny bedroom. Cobwebs covered everything and mouse droppings littered the floor. It looked like no one had used the place for years.

As Paulie walked over to the kitchen area, the silence of the woods was broken by the sound of a car in the distance. He ducked down and listened as the car got closer. Car lights lit up the woods as the car rounded a curve less than a hundred feet from the cabin.

Paulie panicked and ran to the back door, ready to run into the woods. The car continued on. He went back to the front door and walked down a short path to a two lane black top road. He could see tail lights disappearing in the distance. The cabin was not nearly as isolated as he had thought.

Paulie started running down the road in the same direction the car was headed. Relieved that he wasn't lost in the middle of the woods, Paulie had no idea if he was headed in the right direction, but he figured that car had to be going somewhere. He got winded and started to walk.

Paulie walked down the center of the road to stay as far away from the woods as possible. He wondered how often people got killed by bears up here. It must be a common thing, he thought, if this happened to him on his very first time in the forest.

After what seemed to be an hour, Paulie wished another car would come by so he could catch a ride back to town.

He looked down at his suit coat. It was ripped and stained with sweat. His shoes were muddy and his pants were damp.

An hour later, Paulie's feet were killing him and his legs were cramping up. He was freezing. He slapped his arms together to circulate some blood. How could it be so damn cold when it was supposed to be the middle of summer?

Behind him, he heard another car approaching. He turned around to face the car, stepped out into the road and stuck out his thumb. The car was traveling slow. As it approached, he could see an old man hunched behind the wheel. The car drove past him.

"Shit!" Paulie ran a few steps and hollered, "Hey, I need a ride here."

There was a red glow of break lights as the car slowed down and stopped. Paulie ran up to the window. An old man peered out, his face covered with grey whiskers.

"Need a lift, Mister?"

Paulie climbed into the car.

"Where you headed?" the man asked.

"I'm trying to get to Grand View."

"Good, that's where I'm going."

They drove a short way in silence. The old man turned to Paulie, "What's that smell?"

Paulie glanced down at his pants, ignoring him. It took about twenty minutes to reach the outskirts of town. As they drove down Lake Avenue, Paulie asked to get out just past the Freighter View Tavern, where his car was parked.

The old man slowed down as he approached the bar. As they passed the big front windows, Paulie looked in and saw Scott, Joe and that punk kid he was supposed to be following. They were all huddled together talking and laughing. There stood Joe, fine as he could be, and Scott too!

At first, Paulie was puzzled. How could this be? There they were, all laughing together. Slowly he felt his anger building. I bet those assholes are all laughing about me, he thought. The anger exploded in him just like that black bear out in the woods.

"Those bastards!" Paulie screamed.

The old man hit the breaks.

"Stop the car, Grandpa. Stop this damn car!"

"Take it easy, Mister. What's the problem?"

The car lurched to a halt in the middle of Lake Street. Paulie jumped out and slammed the door. The old man pushed down on the accelerator pedal. The car jumped forward, fishtailing down the block, tires squealing.

All conversation came to a stop inside the bar.

"What was that?" Scott said. They all turned to the window. Paulie jumped back into the shadows.

Just up the street, Moon was peddling a girl's bicycle down Lake Street towards the Freighter. He heard tires squealing and looked up to see old man Johnson's car heading straight at him.

Moon pushed down hard on the pedals to get some speed, but it was no use. He leaned the bike over on its side and felt the car sail by, missing him by inches. Moon tumbled from the bike and rolled into a gutter across the street.

Paulie headed down the block back towards his car, his mind racing.

"Them no good dirty bastards," he raged. "They tricked me into going to the woods. There was no bear." He yanked open the car door. "Now they're all getting a good laugh out of this." He pounded on the steering wheel.

"Bastards!"he screamed. Paulie took a deep breath. He clenched his teeth and muttered, "These hicks don't know who they're dealing with. No problem, you assholes. Now, it's my turn".

Moon slowly sat up. He stretched his legs. They seemed to be working. He flexed his arms. His shoulder was scrapped and bleeding but nothing seemed to be broken. He climbed to his feet and picked up the bicycle for support. The handle bars were cocked at a weird angle and the chain was off the sprocket. He pushed the mangled bike over to the Freighter View, leaned it against the building and limped in.

He walked past Scott, Joe and Stephen. Scott took one look at him and asked, "What the hell happened to you?"

"I just got run over by old man Johnson."

"You must be loaded," Joe replied. "Old man Johnson's never driven over thirty miles an hour in his life."

"Well, he did tonight and the old fool almost killed me. Look at me." Moon thrust out his elbow.

His shirt was ripped away and his elbow was scrapped and bleeding.

"You should see the bike. He's gonna pay for a new one, that's for sure!" Moon declared.

Stephen walked over. "Are you okay?"

"I think so. How about getting me a beer?"

Moon smiled and rubbed his shoulder. Stephen saw three brown leaves stuck in his hair.

"I knew this sob story had a purpose," Scott said.

"I'll get you a beer," Stephen replied.

Joe looked over the bar. "Hey, Scottie, see that blonde sitting over there?"

"Yeah."

"She's been staring at me since we walked in here."

"Right, Joe. Like they all do."

"No, I mean it. I'm going to walk over and buy her a drink."

"Geeze, Joe. You're obsessed!"

"Good luck," Stephen said. He turned to Scott, "I better be getting back. I don't think my uncle was too pleased to see me go, so I don't want to stay out too late. But, thanks for the great story. Let's hope our big friend has had enough of Grand View and heads back home."

Moon grabbed the beer, walked over to a group of people he recognized and started telling them about his near death bicycle experience.

"Come here. Let me show you what's left of my bike," Moon said, as he grabbed a disinterested onlooker. They followed Stephen out the door.

Stephen backed the MG out of the angled parking space and headed south on Lake Street.

Paulie watched as Stephen left the bar and got into the car. He started the rental car and pulled out. Paulie began following close behind the MG. He wasn't about to let this kid disappear again.

Moon picked up the mangled bike and was pointing out the damage when he stopped talking mid-sentence. He watched as Stephen drove by in a red MG, with Paulie following close behind.

Stephen noticed bright lights bearing down on him as soon as he pulled out of town. Thinking it could be some drunk behind him, Stephen pressed on the accelerator. The car behind him inched even closer. Stephen punched the accelerator and the MG sped ahead.

The car behind him sped up and then pulled out to pass. Stephen let off the gas to let the maniac driver get by. Instead of passing, the car started moving over towards him. Stephen jerked the wheel hard to the right and headed towards the shoulder. Paulie kept moving the car over and watched as the MG veered off the road into the ditch.

Stephen battled to control the car, but the MG careened down a steep incline and continued moving halfway up an embankment on the other side. The MG rolled over on its side and came to a complete stop buried in a thick clump of bushes. Stephen's head hit the side of the door and he slumped over the steering wheel in a cloud of dirt and leaves.

Paulie slammed to a stop. He grabbed his tool kit and jumped out of the car. He slowly approached the MG. No movement. He walked over to Stephen. Stephen seemed to be knocked out. He grabbed him below the armpits and pulled him from the car. He took a coil of rope from his kit and bound Stephen's hands behind his back. He quickly wrapped a blindfold over Stephen's eyes and then hoisted him into the back seat of his rental car and pushed him down to the floor.

Paulie went back to look at Stephen's car. It had careened into the woods but was still visible from the road. Paulie broke some branches and tossed them over the back of the car making it almost invisible to anyone driving down the road.

He jumped back into his car, checked to make sure Stephen was still out cold, turned around and headed back towards town. Half-way there, Paulie slowed down as it dawned on him that he couldn't take Stephen back to the motel. He had foolishly told Scott and Joe where he was staying. He had to think of some other place to go.

The cabin! It was hidden in the woods and not visible from the road. It was the perfect place to stash Stephen before heading back to New York City. Paulie turned the car around.

Now if he could only remember how to get there.

Chapter 19

Stephen felt cold. It was dark. He tried to move but his head throbbed so badly he had to stop. He felt faint. Stephen tried to reach up and feel his head but his arms would not move. Why couldn't he move them? He drifted back into a light sleep.

Stephen's eyes fluttered. He struggled to stand up but his legs would not cooperate. Another sharp pain at the side of his head brought an end to his attempt. What was happening?

Slowly, memories began to form and Stephen remembered driving away from the Freighter with a car close behind him and then trying to pass. I must have had a car accident. Why can't I move? Am I trapped inside the MG? Stephen struggled to move his arms and legs. He panicked. Nothing was moving freely. He tried to open his eyes wider to get a glimpse of his surroundings. He felt something over his eyes. He blinked and felt cloth rubbing against his eye lashes. He tried to flex his arms. His elbows felt free but he wasn't able to move his wrists. He slowly moved his legs. He could feel his knees move, but not his ankles.

Suddenly it hit him. He was bound and blindfolded! Nothing else made sense. How could he have a car accident and then wake to be tied up and blindfolded? Why had he even gone to GrandView in the first place? He remembered celebrating at the Freighter with

Scott and Joe. His head started to pound again and he felt like he may pass out. His arms and legs ached from being tied, but the pain was concentrated at the side of his head. He stopped moving and closed his eyes. Maybe it would help to dull the pain.

Chapter 20

Jeanette was getting ready for work. She wondered what time Stephen had returned from Grand View. She waited up for him until midnight. When he had not returned, she had gone to bed. She thought it was strange that he would spend so much time in town. There really wasn't that much to do. Was he that upset about the issue with his uncle?

On the way to her office, Jeanette took a quick detour to the garage. She was surprised to see the MG was not there. She turned and walked back to her office. As she approached, she could see Phillip was talking to Bobby.

"Bobby, have you seen the car Stephen used last night?"

"No, Mr. Kahle, I've been making the rounds. The car hasn't been here since Stephen left yesterday."

Phillip turned to Jeanette. "Stephen's not back. I didn't feel comfortable about Stephen going to Grand View alone. We have to do something. We need to find him."

Britt came around the corner and was surprised to see everyone huddled together in conversation. She walked up to Bobby and asked, "What's going on?"

"Stephen went to Grand View yesterday and didn't come home last night."

Britt said, "He's a handsome guy, maybe he found a friend?"

"I doubt that very much," Phillip said tensely. Jeanette saw Bobby stifle a laugh and then she asked, "Phillip, do you want me to call the sheriff's office?"

"No, not yet. Bobby, take the jeep and drive around the back roads surrounding the property and see if you can find the MG. Jeanette, take the truck and drive to Grand View. You know the Henderson's that run the Grand View Campground, don't you?"

"Yes, Scott and I went to school together."

"Stephen mentioned meeting him and somebody named Joe. I'm not sure who that is. Can you drive over to the campground and see if you can find them?"

"I'll leave now," Jeanette said.

Phillip said, "While you do that, I'll take the Porsche and head south on Route 77 and see if I can see any sign of him. Let's get going."

Paulie was excited. He had the kid and now he could get the hell out of this backwater town. He needed to pick up a few groceries and return back to the cabin and wait till it got dark. Then he could sneak back to the motel, pack his things during the night and head out with Stephen before dawn.

Paulie walked over to Stephen and bent down to make sure he was still breathing. He checked the ropes. They were secure. He walked out of the cabin and checked out the perimeter, making sure nobody was around. Once he felt everything was under control, Paulie backed out of the driveway and headed to the store. He picked out a few sandwiches, a bag of chips and a twelve pack of beer. Paulie walked back to the car and put away the bags. He noticed a payphone next to the store and thought it would be a good time to give Al an update. He fed some coins into the phone and dialed Al's number.

"Al, I got the kid. Everything's on plan. We're gonna head back some time before daylight, tomorrow."

"Way to go, Paulie. The boys are going to be surprised. Don't do anything to get yourself pulled over. You better ditch that car you rented and grab yourself another one."

"Okay, Al."

Al hung up and Paulie headed back to the cabin. He was feeling good. Al and the boys were happily surprised. He wished Stephen was in the car with him now so they could just head back to the city. He wasn't looking forward to going back to the cabin in the woods.

Paulie pulled into the narrow driveway and unloaded the groceries. He walked into the living room and was surprised to see Stephen had rolled to a sitting position. The blindfold was still on. Paulie walked over and pulled it off. Dried blood was glued to the left side of Stephen's face and his right eye was starting to turn black. Paulie bent down to see how bad the wound was. There was a small piece of glass embedded in his head from when the MG had hit the ditch. Paulie grabbed the glass and pulled it out. Stephen winced but didn't make a sound.

"You look like hell, kid, but I think you're gonna make it," Paulie commented, as he untied Stephen's hands. He handed Stephen a sandwich. "Eat something."

Stephen took a bite and stared at the man who was standing over him.

"I remember you from the train and from the art gallery, too. You've been following me since I left New York. Why?"

"It's your old man, kid. He loves to play the ponies, but he don't like to pay. He owes the boys a shit load of dough. Your old man finds out I got you, you better hope he changes his mind. Right?"

Paulie walked to the kitchen and returned with two cold beers. He popped them both open and handed one to Stephen.

"Here, kid. Look, for me this is just a job, okay? Nothing personal. My boss tells me to do something, I do it. You got a little banged up, but I think you're fine. We gotta get you the hell out of here and get us both back to New York. And if you ask me, it can't be too soon. Your old man pays, you go home. Easy as pie."

Stephen heard what Paulie was saying, but it was hard to comprehend. He knew his father went to the track occasionally, but he had no idea he had a gambling problem.

Chapter 21

Bobby was driving down Pine Ridge Road, almost to the intersection of Route 77 when he saw someone on a bicycle heading his way. Bobby pulled up next to him and motioned for him to stop.

"Hey, Moo...ahh...Francis, where you headed?"

"I'm on my way to the gate so I can get some picketing money."

"Picketing money?"

"Yeah, we get paid a buck fifty an hour to stand outside the gate and wave a damn sign. You can't beat that."

Bobby wondered who the hell was bankrolling that but instead he asked, "Mr. Kahle's nephew didn't come back from Grand View last night. You ever met him? Do you know where he could be?"

"Yeah, I met the guy. He bought me a beer at The Freighter. He seems okay, but no, I don't know where he is."

"If you hear anything, let me know. I'm sure Mr. Kahle would make it worth your while, if you know what I mean."

Bobby drove off and watched in his rear view mirror as Moon resumed peddling the bicycle towards the gate. Abruptly Moon stopped. He turned the bicycle around and headed back in the direction he came from. Moon was thinking to hell with this buck fifty an hour bullshit job. I should be able to make some real money now!

Jeanette pulled into the Grand View Campground and walked up to the office. She asked if Scott was working and was directed to look for him behind a partially constructed recreation hall.

Scott was on his knees, holding a level, as Joe was pounding in a stake next to a 2-by-4 footing. King was panting in the shade of a huge red oak tree. Scott glanced up and saw Jeanette walking towards them. She had a worried look.

"Hi, Jeanette. What brings you to the campground?"

"You met Stephen, Mr. Kahle's nephew, right, Scott?"

Joe threw down his hammer and walked towards Scott and Jeanette.

"Yeah, we've met him. Seems like a nice guy, why? What's the matter?"

"Well, he didn't come home last night. He had Mr. Kahle's MG and left unexpectedly for Grand View. We looked all over Cliffside Manor and he didn't return."

"Oh, shit," Scott muttered.

"What?" Jeanette asked.

Scott and Joe explained how they had been watching out for the person Stephen thought was following him and how they had set up a prank to give the guy a good scare, hoping that would be enough to get him to go back to where he came from.

They explained how they had called Stephen and asked him to come by the Freighter for a drink so they could let him in on what happened. The last time they saw Stephen was around ten thirty the night before when he left the bar to return to Cliffside Manor.

"Maybe our little prank wasn't such a good idea," Joe said.

"You can't second guess what's already happened," Jeanette said. "We have to do something about finding Stephen and we need to do it now."

"Why don't we head over to The Freighter and start there," Scott proposed. "That's the last place we saw Stephen."

They all piled into Scott's car, including King, and headed into town. Scott pulled up to the front of the bar.

"Okay, what now?" Joe asked.

Scott said, "When Stephen left, he told us he was heading back to Cliffside Manor. Let's retrace his steps and see if we can see anything on the way."

Scott pulled out onto Lake Street and they slowly headed out of town, following Route 77. Jeanette and Joe watched the road to the right while Scott took the left. Scott drove slowly, nobody was talking.

As they got to an area half a mile before the intersection of Pine Ridge Road and Route 77, Joe yelled, "Scott, stop the car!"

Scott slammed on the brakes and pulled off onto the shoulder.

"What did you see?" Scott asked.

Joe jumped out of the car and headed towards the ditch, King at his heels.

"Look, deep tire tracks going off the shoulder in the mud."

Scott and Jeanette scrambled behind him. Joe was following the tracks as they lead up the ditch and into the woods.

"I found the car!" Joe yelled.

Scott and Jeanette were right behind him.

"Look at it!" Jeanette said. "Something slammed into the driver's side. There's blood!"

Scott and Joe ran over to the smashed driver's side window. They could clearly see the blood stains. Scott walked along the shoulder of the road examining two sets of car tracks.

Scott said, "Someone forced Stephen off the road. It has to be that New York guy, Paulie. Joe, this is close to the road we took Paulie down when we played that trick on him."

Chapter 22

Paulie was sitting in the living room area working on his fourth beer. Stephen was feeling a little better after having had something to eat.

There was a rustling noise from the woods. Paulie jumped up. What was that? Paulie ran to the bunk beds and came back holding his gun. He ducked down under the open kitchen window and slowly rose, peeking over the sill. He planted his legs wide and held the revolver with both hands. He peered out the window into the woods. The bushes quivered and a huge porcupine strolled out of the underbrush, heading towards the cabin. Paulie had never seen anything like it.

The spiny creature slowly ambled through the leaves towards the back porch of the cabin. Paulie reacted instinctively. He aimed and pulled the trigger. A shot rang out, piercing the silence. The porcupine squealed, flew up into the air in a backwards somersault, and landed behind some bushes.

Stephen stiffened. Was someone coming to rescue him? He stumbled to his feet, his legs still bound together, and peered out of the window.

"What was it?" Stephen asked.

"Some wild animal was heading towards the back door," Paulie muttered. He thought to himself how do people live out here?

Scott, Joe and Jeanette all hit the ground when the shot rang out.

"Was someone shooting at us?" Joe asked.

"I don't know, it sounded very close," Scott replied.

Jeanette slowly rose to her knees and looked over to where the sound came from. "I think it came from Peterson's camp," she said.

"Let's find out," Scott said, "but don't take the road. Head through the woods."

Scott grabbed King's collar so he wouldn't get too far ahead and they started to move slowly through the trees. As they approached the cabin clearing, Scott motioned for them to stop.

"Look, there's a car parked on the side of the house."

Scott said to Jeanette, "You stay and watch from here. Joe, go around to the other side of the cabin, but stay in the woods. I'll go check out the back and we'll meet here."

He looked at the dog, "King, stay." The dog immediately sat at Jeanette's feet.

Joe and Scott disappeared into the woods, each taking different paths. They proceeded slowly and quietly, making sure not to snap any limbs or twigs. Years of hunting experience kicked in.

Twenty minutes later, they returned to Jeanette. Joe whispered, "The car behind the cabin is a rental. It's got some damage on the passenger side. Paint scrapes match the color on the MG. Stephen's standing by the window and Paulie is sitting in a chair drinking a beer. He has a gun."

Jeanette said, "We need to go and get the police."

"We don't have time. You said it was time to do something, remember?" Scott said. "A pane of glass is busted out of the back door. Jeanette, you stay here and watch the front door. Joe and I will sneak over to the back. We need to surprise Paulie and get Stephen out."

Scott and Joe disappeared back into the woods. They made their way to the clearing behind the cabin and stopped to observe.

Joe heard something move in the bushes and froze. Scott turned to see where the sound was coming from. The foliage parted and a bloody porcupine limped out of the brush, dragging its hind leg. It ambled into the clearing, heading back towards the cabin.

From a distance, Jeanette watched as a porcupine waddled out into the clearing. King sniffed the air and jumped to his feet. The hair on the back of his neck stood up straight. He let out a bark and flew full speed through the woods towards the bleeding porcupine.

Hearing more commotion, Paulie jumped from the chair, knocking over his can of beer. He ran to the living room window and saw a big blur rushing towards the cabin.

Stephen heard Paulie scream, "It's a wolf!" He saw Paulie take aim and fire the gun right through the window.

Hearing a shot from the inside the cabin, Scott and Joe ran from the woods and burst through the back door.

Paulie spun from the window, aiming the gun towards the noise. Scott threw himself at Paulie, hitting him in the chest. Paulie was knocked off his feet and fell squarely on Scott. Joe raced over and tried to wrestle the gun from his grip.

"I've got him, Scotty."

Paulie squeezed off two rounds as he struggled with Joe. One bullet thumped into a wall behind Stephen. The other bullet shattered a mirror in the kitchen. King barked, ran past the porcupine and jumped into the cabin through the shattered living room window. The dog leapt over Joe, sunk his teeth deep into Paulie's gun hand, and shook his head back and forth. Paulie let out a piercing scream as the gun slid into a corner of the living room.

"Get him off me!" Paulie hollered.

Scott commanded, "King, sit." As Joe ran over and picked up the gun, King let go of Paulie's hand, took a step back and sat down. Joe pointed the gun at Paulie. "Don't move."

Stephen jumped over a toppled chair and tossed Scott the rope that had recently been around his arms.

"Use this to tie him up."

Chapter 23

Phillip came out of the office shaking his head, while Britt sat on the leather couch filing her nails.

"I just got off the phone with Martin. I had to tell him about Stephen. As usual with Martin, there always seems to be a little more to the story than meets the eye."

"What's his story this time?" Britt asked, afraid to hear the answer.

"Now he tells me there was another reason he wanted Stephen to come up and stay with me. At first, he told me how nice it would be for Stephen to get away from the city and have him try and forget about his old girlfriend before he goes to off to school in the fall."

"That wasn't the case?" Britt asked.

"Partly true, but more importantly, Martin actually wanted to get him out of there because he had collected some gambling debts he couldn't repay."

"This sounds serious. How bad is it?" Britt asked.

"I'm not sure. Martin has always enjoyed gambling. He loves playing the horses. From what he told me, his gambling got out of hand and he's in trouble with his bookies. I tried to find out what kind of debt he was talking about, but when Martin heard Stephen was missing, he went to pieces and the conversation ended," Phillip sighed.

"He is also having problems with his latest play. It's not coming together as quickly as he thought. He was due another check when he delivered the first draft."

Britt lit a cigarette. "If the play was done on time, he would have had money to fix his problem, right?"

"Exactly. That was what he was counting on to pay off his debts. When that didn't happen, things got out of control fast. Bookies don't like not getting paid. They want their money. Stephen's just being used as a guarantee at this point."

The phone rang in Jeanette's office. Phillip walked across the hall and picked it up. Britt poured herself a brandy from the decanter on the bar and took a sip.

"I can't believe this!" Phillip said as he walked back into the trophy room.

"Is it about Stephen?" Britt asked.

"No, you won't believe the timing on this. It was my brokers in Hollywood. They finally want to talk to me about funding for the next picture."

"That's wonderful!" Britt exclaimed.

"How is that wonderful?" Phillip frowned. "With Stephen missing, I can't go now!"

Chapter 24

Paulie was hunched forward in the backseat of the car as Scott drove back to Grand View. Paulie's hands were tied behind his back. Joe sat next to him with Paulie's revolver pointed at his chest. Stephen was squeezed in next to Joe. Jeanette and King were in the front passenger seat.

Paulie stared sullenly out the window. He was trying to think how many times had he been tied up before. Was it two or three? He remembered the first time was when the Bewinski brothers ambushed him near Coney Island. They tied his hands behind his back and beat him to a pulp with a pipe.

The second time was when those three Puerto Ricans jumped him. Again, they tied him up and gave him a hell of a beating. That was the first time his nose got broken. He remembered how Al laughed like hell when he heard about it.

Al pulled him aside and said, "Why you letting those punks beat you up like that? Look at your nose. Paulie, you're gonna lose your good looks if you keep this up. Let me show you a little trick for next time."

Al got a piece of rope. As he was tying Paulie's hands behind his back, he showed him how to lock his fingers and keep the palms of his hands pushed out a ways. Paulie tried it and sure enough, when he squeezed his hands together, the bindings became loose enough to work off his wrists.

Paulie turned from the window.

"You hicks don't know who you're messing with here," he said. "Believe me, the best thing for everyone is to let me take the kid back to the city, my guys get paid and he waltzes home. This way everybody's happy and no one gets hurt."

As he was speaking, Paulie pushed his hands together and tried Al's trick. Sure enough, he felt the ropes loosen. He squeezed his hands together tighter and moved his little finger up to the bottom strand of rope. Paulie pulled steadily and felt the rope slip off. He gave a slight shake and another strand fell down, freeing his hands.

Scott laughed. "If you think we're going to hand over our friend to the likes of you, mister, you got another thing coming. We'll drop your ass off at the Sheriff's office and they can sort this out. Attempted murder, kidnapping and breaking and entering should keep them busy with you for quite a while."

"No shit!" Joe said, glancing at Scott.

This was just the opening Paulie was looking for. He shot his left hand over and grabbed Joe's gun hand. He punched Joe hard in the face and wrenched the gun free. Blood poured from Joe's nose.

Jeanette screamed, "He's got the gun!"

Scott swerved onto the gravel shoulder of the road. As the car was slowing to a stop, Scott turned to Stephen and motioned for him to get out. Stephen opened the passenger door, jumped out, and ran up a hillside into the woods. As the car came to a dusty halt, Paulie jumped out holding the gun. He shouted, "Everybody out."

He looked around. "Where's the kid?"

Everything had happened so fast, only Scott knew Stephen had tumbled out of the car and had run into the woods. Scott ran over to Joe. Blood was coming from his nose.

Scott was furious. He glared at Joe, "I thought you tied him up?"

"I did, I tied him up real good," Joe said, as he held his sleeve up to his nose.

Paulie laughed, "I told you, you didn't know who you were dealing with. Next time you tie someone up, you dumb shit, check their hands. You could have driven a truck through mine."

Paulie looked around again. "Where the hell is the kid?" he yelled. He pointed the gun to Joe's head. "You get me the kid or I shoot."

Scott took a step forward.

"Stand back," Paulie said. "I need that kid."

Joe was upset Scott thought it was his fault Paulie got loose. Joe took a flying leap towards Paulie. Paulie took a step back and fired. A bullet hit Joe and he crumpled on the ground.

Jeanette watched as a jeep came over the hill and headed full speed straight towards the group. Jeanette recognized the vehicle as Uncle Phillip's and Bobby was driving.

Paulie watched as the car approached. He kept the gun pointed at the assembly and stepped backwards towards Scott's car, which was still running. He jumped into the driver's seat, punched the gas and sprayed gravel along the road. Tires squealed as they hit the blacktop.

Stephen watched from a crouched position in the woods. As Paulie and the car drove off, Stephen emerged and rejoined the group.

Bobby and Scott bent over Joe.

"He took a shot to the shoulder, it's bleeding pretty bad," Bobby said. "We need to get an ambulance."

He jumped into the jeep and started talking on the two way radio. Bobby and Scott held a towel on Joe's wound. After a few minutes, the faint wail of a siren could be heard in the distance.

Paulie drove through Grand View, heading to his motel room. He knew the heat would be turned on now. He needed to find another place to lay low. Paulie slowly cruised past the motel complex looking for any sign of the cops. Nothing looked out of the ordinary. Why should it, he thought. The kid and the rest of the group should still be standing on the side of the road. Paulie continued driving a mile past the motel and then turned into the entrance of a county boat launch. He parked Scott's car in the middle of a group of trucks and boat trailers and walked back to the motel.

As he approached, Paulie scanned the parking lot again. He unlocked the door to his room and pulled out his suitcase. He opened the closet and started pulling suits from their hangers. Paulie was reaching for his snake skin shoes when he heard a sound behind him. He turned to see the bathroom door swing open. Paulie pulled the gun from his belt.

"Cool it, Paulie. It's me, Moonie. I'm on your side, buddy, calm down. I'm here to help you."

Chapter 25

Phillip was in his office when he got the call from Bobby that Stephen had been found. They were all at the Sheriff's office, explaining what had happened. Phillip walked quickly over to Britt's place.

"Britt, Stephen's been found. I'm headed to Grand View. Have Cora make something to eat in case Stephen is hungry when we get back."

At the sheriff's office, Phillip heard about Paulie taking Stephen to the cabin. He heard how Scott, Jeanette and Joe were able to rescue Stephen. He learned how Joe got shot and how Paulie managed to get away.

As they pulled into the driveway of Cliffside Manor, Britt came rushing out the front door. Stephen got out of the car. Britt ran up and threw her arms around him.

"Oh, Stephen! We're so glad you're back safe and sound." She pulled his head back and gave him a kiss. Uncle Phillip, Jeanette and Bobby all looked on in amazement.

Stephen gently pushed Britt away. He wiped the lipstick from his face and stepped back with a puzzled look. Britt laughed and walked over to Phillip. There was an awkward silence before Phillip turned to Bobby and said, "I want you here around the clock. I'm also going to hire another guard. We can't afford to have him disappear again."

He turned to Stephen, "You must stay at Cliffside Manor at all times. If you go anywhere, you go with us as a group. Cora has put out something to eat. Let's go to the dining room and try and get back to our normal routine."

After dinner, Phillip, Britt, Jeanette and Stephen retired to the trophy room.

"Stephen, when you disappeared, I called your parents. I spoke to your father and it seems there was another reason you were sent away this summer, besides your girlfriend issue. I'm sure you don't know this, but your father thinks his gambling may have been behind this problem."

"I know, Uncle. That creep Paulie told me what happened."

"Well, tomorrow I'll call your father and arrange to have whatever money he owes paid so you're no longer in danger."

Phillip addressed the whole group. "We all need to be very careful and not mention this to anyone. We have to keep this nasty business out of the papers. Neither Stephen's father nor I need to have this kind of publicity. It wouldn't be good for his reputation or mine."

Britt walked over to the cocktail table in front of Stephen and leaned over to freshen her drink. Her blouse was cut low and she seemed to linger until she made sure Stephen noticed.

Uncle Phillip broke the silence. "Stephen, I received the call I was waiting for from California. I hate to leave you after all you have been through, but it looks like the funding is coming together for my next picture. I must take a few days and get this business wrapped up in Los Angeles."

"I understand, Uncle Phillip. Don't worry, I'll be fine. I'll be sticking close to home and I'm sure nothing else is going to happen."

Stephen turned to Britt, "Will you be going with Uncle Phillip to California?"

"No, dear boy. Phillip wants me to go, but I've put Hollywood behind me and...," Britt paused, "someone has to be here to watch over you."

Phillip ignored her comment and looked over to Jeanette. "Now that Stephen's home, can you call and make my plane reservations tonight. I'll try to be back in three or four days. But for now, we're celebrating your safe return. Let me get everyone another round of drinks!"

Phillip went around the room and filled Jeanette's glass, got Stephen and Britt another drink and handed Bobby, who was sitting near the door, a beer.

The talk turned to Hollywood and how difficult it was to finance movies these days. Britt had everyone laughing when she told a story about how the grandson from a family known for 'old money' almost got kicked out of the will once his relatives learned he had backed one of her "B" movies with a million dollar guarantee.

After a few drinks, everyone seemed to be loosening up from the unbearable tension of the last few days. Phillip was laughing hard at something Jeanette had said. Britt walked over and turned on the stereo. Loud music started pounding from recessed speakers. Britt walked over and tugged on Stephen's shirt to get his attention and pointed across the room.

"Look how relieved your uncle is, now that you're back unharmed. Stephen, I know what you went through was harrowing, but Phillip was beside himself with worry." Britt snuggled closer. "I hope you understand he isn't the only one celebrating your return."

Britt's perfume welled up on Stephen. He felt her soft curves push close to him. The drinks had relaxed him into a mellow mood. Britt felt so warm next to him.

"Thank you, Britt. I'm happy to be here safe and sound and in one piece. I just hope Joe is okay."

Uncle Phil walked over to the stereo and switched it off.

"We've all had a very trying time these last few days. Since I have to be up early tomorrow morning, I'm calling it a night. Good night Stephen. Good night, Jeanette."

He turned to Britt, "Let's go, Britt."

"Go? I don't have to get up early. The party's just getting started!"

"I think you've had enough to drink, darling. Come along, now."

Phillip reached for Britt's arm.

Britt made no attempt to get up. Phillip was visibly upset, but he controlled his emotions.

"As you will, Britt," Phillip stated. He wheeled around and walked out. An uncomfortable silence descended upon the room.

Stephen stood up and said, "Yeah, I'm exhausted too." He turned to Britt and Jeanette, "I'll see you tomorrow morning for coffee. Good night."

Stephen left the trophy room while Britt was pouring herself another drink. Bobby stood guard just outside the door. Jeanette followed Stephen into the hallway.

Chapter 26

"How'd you get in here?" Paulie growled. The barrel of his gun was pointing at Moon's chest.

"Calm down, Paulie. I know the desk clerk. We're pals. Put the gun down, will you?"

Paulie didn't move.

"Like I said, I'm only here to help you. The skinny guy in the office works the picket line with me every Wednesday at Kahle's place. I told him you and me was tight and he let me in."

Moon sat down on the edge of the bed. Paulie's gun followed him.

"The other night at the Freighter, I seen you follow Kahle's nephew when he left the bar. The next day everyone's in a panic because the kid didn't make it home. I asked my friend on the picket line to keep an eye out and let me know if anything happens. Hey, can you put the goddamn gun down?"

"Keep talking," Paulie said, not moving the gun.

"He gave me a call a little while ago saying Mr. Kahle just drove in with his nephew in the car. So I put two and two together and figured you might need my help just about now."

"And how is it you're gonna help me?" Paulie asked.

"Oh, that's easy, but can you put the gun down? It's hard to think when all I can see is that barrel pointing at me."

Paulie moved the gun slightly.

"Okay, thanks. Now, where do I start? First, you ain't from around here, and everyone can tell. You stick out like a sore thumb with them suits, your fancy shoes and the way you talk."

Paulie glanced down at his shoes.

"We both know you grabbed the kid. So by now your rental car is hotter than that gun you're holding. The cops will be swarming this place in a matter of minutes and you don't even got a bicycle you could ride out of town on."

"And I ain't using yours, if that's what you're thinking," Paulie responded.

"Very funny, you want me to go on?"

Moon stood up. "The way I look at it, Paulie, you need a friend and you need one right away. And I mean now, right now."

Paulie glared at Moon for a second and asked, "So what can you do for me, sport?"

"Plenty. First we got to get out of here. You can bunk down at my place till the heats off. Then, for part of the action, I can deliver Stephen on a silver platter and you can get the hell out of Grand View with a car I get for you."

"No shit. Ain't you the resourceful one? Just how much is all this friendship gonna to cost me?"

Moon thought for a moment. He was trying to think of a number good enough to make it worth his while, but not high enough to piss this guy off.

"Two grand ought to do the trick."

"Screw you," Paulie sneered, "you ask for two grand, that tells me you really want five hundred and you'd probably shit your pants if I gave you two bills."

Paulie took a menacing step towards Moon and pushed him back down in the chair.

"I'll tell you what, Mr. Moon. If you can do all the shit you think you can, you and me will be best buddies and I'll throw you four hundred bucks for your trouble."

"Four hundred?" Moonie was not happy. This was not the kind of payday he anticipated, but then again, he was standing in a darkened motel room with a pissed off New York mobster holding a gun. Moonie decided his negotiating was probably over.

"Paulie, you just got yourself a deal. Grab your shit. We got to get the hell out of here now."

Paulie resumed stuffing his suits into his suitcase. He didn't take time to fold them neatly; he just crumpled them in, one on top of the other. He reached under the bed and slid out his butterfly collecting kit.

"What's that?" Moon asked.

"None of you damn business, is what that is," Paulie shot back.

After ten more minutes of rummaging, Paulie had all his belongings packed and was ready to go.

Moon said, "I'm gonna walk outside and make sure nobody's hanging around eyeballing us."

Moon cracked open the motel room door and stepped out. He glanced around. A steady background noise of peeping frogs and chirping crickets was coming from the woods. The only other sound he could hear was a buzzing sound as the T in the MOTEL sign flickered on and off. Moon walked the whole length of the motel, front and back, to make sure no cops were watching the place.

He returned to the room, pushed open the door and said, "Okay, let's get out of here."

As they drove over to Moon's place, Paulie said, "I never seen you in a car before. You're always on a bicycle. I thought you didn't have a car."

"I don't. This is my neighbors. She fell down and broke her hip, so I take her car and buy her groceries. She gives me a few bucks. When I need the car, I can use it, but she dont't like it when I drive it too much, so mostly, I ride a bike."

They pulled up to a three story yellow brick building. Green paint was peeling off the window frames. Moon jumped out. "This is it."

Paulie grabbed his suitcases and they both headed for the door.

"I'm up on the third floor."

"Where's the goddamned elevator?" Paulie asked.

"Very funny, this ain't the city and there ain't no elevator. We hoof the stairs."

Moon reached down and grabbed one of Paulie's bags. Paulie and Moon grunted their way up to the third floor.

Paulie thought the place smelled like a combination of old french fry grease and sour cabbage. They finally got to the landing. Moon's room was the third one down, on the right. Moon put down Paulie's bag and fumbled for his keys. The door swung open and they stepped in.

Paulie looked around. Piles of clothes, magazines, bicycle parts and a pile of black feathers littered the room. Paulie threw his suitcases on the floor and grabbed Moon by both shoulders.

"What kind of shit-hole is this?" Paulie shouted. "You want me to stay in this dump?"

Moon's eyes opened wide. "Hey, hey, calm down. Not so loud, you wanna upset all the neighbors? I didn't have a lot of time to clean up my place for taking you in. Give me a few minutes and I'll pick up some of this shit."

Moon motioned for Paulie to sit in a shabby green corduroy chair. Moon swept a pile of magazines off the seat cushion and picked up a dirty blanket that was hanging from the back of the chair.

Paulie brushed off the cushion with his hand and eased into the chair. Moon scurried around the apartment picking up assorted clothing and attending to scattered piles of clutter. He worked his way over to a card table set up under a window. He picked up a cup of cold coffee that was sitting next to a dead bird and headed to the kitchen sink.

"What the hell is that?" Paulie called out from the chair.

"Oh, just a cup of old coffee from this morning."

"Not the coffee, you asshole. What's that shit on the table?"

"Oh, that? It's a crow. That other stuff is my taxidermy tools. I sent away for a home study course and I'm learning how to stuff birds and small animals."

Paulie said, "What!"

"Don't laugh. It's a lot harder than I thought. Once I get the hang of it, I can make some good money around here as a certified taxidermist."

"Listen here, Norman Bates junior, I got a notion to stuff you for bringing me into this filthy garbage pit!"

Moon ignored Paulie's rant and continued to scurry around the room straightening things.

Paulie got up from the chair and walked around the room.

"Where's the bedrooms?"

"There ain't none. This is a rooming house and I only got one room. The couch pulls out and you can sleep there."

"With you?" Paulie asked. "I ain't sleeping with you."

"No, you get the bed and I'll sleep on a sleeping bag over there on the floor."

"Where's the bathroom?"

"It's down the hall. I share it with the other people who live on this floor."

Paulie shook his head. He needed to grab the kid as soon as possible and get the hell out of this dump.

Moon tossed a pile of papers into a can under the sink.

"Why don't you get settled in? You can hang up your clothes in my closet. I'm gonna run up to the store and pick up some beer and cigarettes."

Once Moon left, Paulie took the opportunity to examine Moon's small, cluttered room more closely. He could hear a television set playing from the next room and a radio was on a few doors away.

Paulie walked over to the table near the window and looked at the dead bird and taxidermy tools. He bent over the table and saw there were actually three bird corpses. All appeared to be failed attempts to be stuffed into any recognizable forms. Piles of cotton and stiff wires were sticking out of them. They were twisted in grotesque shapes and one appeared to be turned inside out. Paulie stepped back and coughed. A strong chemical smell combined with a hint of decay was coming from the table.

Paulie noticed a phone mounted on the wall by a small refrigerator. Maybe he better check in with Al.

"Al, Paulie here." There was silence. "Al, you there?"

Al growled into the phone. "You got the kid, right?" Paulie could tell Al was not happy.

"Well, I had the kid…"

"Had the kid? What's going on Paulie, the boys…"

Paulie interrupted, "Yea, I had the damn kid but his pals busted him out. I shot a guy and the heats on. I had to find a new place to stay. That's why I'm calling. We, I mean, there's a new plan and I should have him back by tomorrow or the next day."

The phone was silent for a moment then Paulie could hear Al breathing.

"Look, Paulie. The man's getting tired of waiting. You need to show up here with that kid now. I'm getting heat for sending you, after all your screw ups. If you don't grab that kid, I'd suggest you don't come back at all. You might just want to stay wherever you're at permanently."

"No, Al, it's okay. I got a plan and I'm headed out soon. Believe me, I can't wait to get back. Everything's gonna be great."

"Don't mess this up. You got three days, no more." Al slammed down the phone.

Chapter 27

The next morning, Stephen woke up and glanced at the clock on the nightstand. It was almost nine o'clock. No wonder it was so light in his room. He stretched and felt muscles pull in his legs and back, instantly reminding him of what had happened.

Stephen snuggled down deeper into the covers. He caught a whiff of Britt's perfume on his face. Stephen breathed a sigh of relief that he was back in the safety of the mansion. He fell back to sleep.

At twenty minutes after nine, Stephen woke again and got out of bed. He showered and put on some sweat pants and a sweat shirt. It always seemed cold in the mansion in the morning, no matter what the weather was like outside.

Jeanette was eating breakfast alone in the dining room. Stephen helped himself to the breakfast buffet Cora had set out in the kitchen and joined Jeanette.

"Did Uncle Philip get off okay this morning?" Stephen asked.

"Yes, the car service picked him up bright and early at six thirty. This is a very important meeting for him. I hope all goes well."

"I wonder if I should just go back home," Stephen stated.

Jeanette seemed startled. "Why would you say that?"

"Well, look what a bother I've been. My uncle's girlfriend keeps flirting with me. Someone pushes me over a cliff and then

I'm kidnapped. I meet some new friends and one of them gets shot and is in the hospital."

"Stephen, your uncle couldn't wait till you got here. I know how excited he was to spend time with you."

"Yeah, that was before I got here. Besides, Uncle Phillip has a business to run. If you and the guys hadn't been able to rescue me, he would have had to stay here and miss his important meeting. Look at the worry I've put him through the last few days," Stephen said, toying with his food.

"Your uncle is going to take care of the issue that caused all those troubles, so things should be just fine from now on."

Stephen didn't say anything, he just nodded.

Jeanette looked Stephen directly in the eye. "Something else is bothering you. I could tell when we had our little party last night. You seemed preoccupied."

Stephen looked surprised. He hesitated and then said, "You're right. Something is bothering me."

"What?"

"I should have never run into the woods," Stephen sighed.

"What are you talking about?"

"When Paulie got loose and Scott was slowing down the car, he told me to jump out and run."

"I know, what was wrong with that?" Jeanette asked with a puzzled look.

"I ran away! I left all my friends with a mobster holding a gun. This was my problem, not anybody else's."

"Stephen, think about it. Scott had a brilliant move. Paulie was after you. Once we all got out of the car he was completely confused when he didn't see you. He didn't know what to do. That's why he took off when Bobby showed up."

"But I ran out on my friends. Can you imagine what it felt like when I heard Paulie tell Joe about how he got out of his bindings and then watched as Joe jumped him and then got shot?"

"You couldn't help that!" Jeanette exclaimed.

"I should have been there so we could have all confronted him. Scott, Joe and I could have taken him on."

Jeanette hugged him again. "Stephen, that's ridiculous. Think about this. If you were there with us, Paulie, who was the only one with a gun, could have shoved you into the car, shot all of us and had you back in New York with the mob by now."

Stephen paused. "I never thought of that."

"Well, you should have. By the way, on a happier note, Scott called while you were sleeping. Joe's going to be fine. He will have his arm in a sling for awhile, but it should heal just like new."

"That's good," Stephen said, with relief.

"Oh, and Scott suggested that you don't try and see Joe right now."

"Really! Why, because it would be too dangerous?"

"No," Jeanette laughed. "Because there were way too many girls in his room. When Scott tried to see Joe he couldn't even squeeze in. He had to leave and come back later."

Jeanette watched as Stephen started to laugh.

"You just need to relax, forget about what happened and start enjoying life at the mansion. You have the whole summer to look forward to."

"Well, I do want to stay," Stephen said, looking at Jeanette. "I hope you're right."

"So what are your plans for today?" Jeanette asked.

"The first thing on my plate is thanking you for putting yourself in danger and coming to my rescue."

Stephen leaned over and gave Jeanette a long hug. He closed his eyes and marveled at how good she felt in his arms. Jeanette did not pull away. Her body felt good next to him. After several moments, he released her. She looked into his eyes and he could see a tear running down her cheek.

"What's wrong?"

She dabbed at her cheek with her napkin and broke into a soft laugh.

"Oh, nothing's wrong. Nothing at all. I'm just so glad you're back." She paused, "Well, that was a great start to your day. Now, what else do you have planned?"

"I thought I would spend the day exploring the library. It looks like you could spend a lifetime up there and still not uncover everything. It would be nice if you could join me."

"I've got a few things to do this morning, but how about if I meet you up there early afternoon?"

"That would be perfect."

Stephen went to his room and took his drawing pad and charcoals to the library. He found some art books featuring the old masters and began sketching. He lost himself in his drawings until pangs of hunger made him pause. He glanced at the library clock across from his uncle's oil portrait. It was nearly one o'clock. No wonder he was hungry. Stephen headed down to the dining room. The room was empty, so he walked down the hall to Jeanette's office.

"Lunch time?"

She was busy at her desk and looked up when she heard him.

"Is it that time already? Yes, I'm hungry."

Jeanette and Stephen walked to the kitchen. Cora was busy pulling pies out of the oven.

"What delicious treat do you have for lunch today, Cora?" Jeanette asked.

Cora looked up from the oven, her glasses covered with steam. She said, "Italian beef sandwiches with a salad, picked from the garden, and a fresh strawberry/rhubarb pie that just came out of the oven."

"Wonderful!" Stephen exclaimed.

During lunch, Jeanette asked Stephen what he had occupied his time with up in the library. He explained he had been sketching pictures from the old masters. Jeanette mentioned that she had a few more things to do, but it looked like she could join him around three, if that was alright.

Stephen thought to himself it would be more than alright but instead said, "Sure, but only if you will let me draw you. I'm tired of trying to duplicate those dumpy old women in the old master's pictures."

Jeanette laughed and said, "Draw me! I don't think so. There must be many more beautiful things you can illustrate besides me."

Stephen blurted out, "I doubt that!" and then realized he probably said more than he wanted to. He continued, "No, I think it would be fun to see if I can capture your personality, but if it would make you feel uncomfortable, we don't have to."

"I don't mind. But only if you have patience with me since I've never done anything like this before and I'm going to feel very self-conscious."

Jeanette finished her lunch, got up and put her dishes in the sink. She returned to her office and went back to her work, all the time thinking about meeting Stephen in the afternoon. She straightened up her desk, went back to her room and tried on several different outfits. She ended up selecting a beautiful lace dress. The dress was black, sleeveless, with a lace overlay and decorated with beads. She quickly put on some make-up, pulled her air up in a twist and headed up to the library.

Stephen was so busy preparing a new sheet of paper on his sketchpad, he didn't notice when she walked in.

"I hope you like my new look!" Jeanette said nervously. Stephen glanced up.

At first, Stephen didn't recognize that it was Jeanette standing in front of him. She was stunning. Stephen just stood there. After a few long seconds, he felt like a complete idiot.

Stephen stammered, "You, you look beautiful, Jeanette. Now, I only hope I can do you justice!"

The hours melted away as Jeanette posed and Stephen sketched. She was amazed at how talented he was. She had never seen any of his work before and seeing herself as his inspiration was very thrilling. As Stephen was finishing a third sketch of Jeanette, the library clock chimed five times.

"Come and see, Jeanette."

For this sketch, Stephen had Jeanette sit in a retro pinup type pose with her hands resting on her knees. Jeanette gazed at the beautifully illustrated picture. She knew it was her, but found it hard to believe Stephen could capture her likeness with such a soft and beautiful spirit.

"I love it! I think it's my favorite one. But you forgot one thing."

Stephen inspected the drawing. "What did I forget?"

"You forgot to sign it, silly."

"Oh, it's only a sketch," Stephen dismissed with a laugh.

"No, it's MY sketch and I want you to sign it for me."

Stephen scribbled his signature on the bottom, tore it off his sketch pad and handed it to her.

"I had a wonderful time," he said. "I hope you did to."

Jeanette leaned into him. Stephen wrapped his arms around her. Jeanette looked up and Stephen kissed her. The kiss was long.

It was like they had both wanted this and once it happened, neither wanted it to stop.

Jeanette said, "Do you do this to all your models?"

"You're my only model," Stephen replied.

Jeanette helped Stephen pack up his supplies and store them back in his room. They held hands as they walked downstairs towards the kitchen.

Cora was in the process of setting out a roast beef dinner with mashed potatoes and green beans. Stephen and Jeanette fixed their plates and moved to the dining room to eat.

Stephen poured two glasses of merlot. Cora entered the dinning room with some hot rolls just out of the oven.

"Cora, have you seen Britt today?" Jeanette asked.

"No, I thought she may have changed her mind and gone to California with Mr. Kahle."

Jeanette said, "I was up helping Mr. Kahle get ready for his trip and he was the only one using the car service to the airport. It's not like Britt to stay at her place all day without coming over to the mansion. We all know she doesn't cook. Is Bobby around?"

Cora said, "No, the last time I saw Bobby was around ten o'clock when I saw him talking to those annoying protesters at the gate."

"If Britt doesn't show up for supper, Stephen and I will walk over and see if she is all right."

Jeanette and Stephen continued to eat, expecting Britt to breeze in at any moment.

After the meal, Cora set down two pieces of warm strawberry/ rhubarb pie.

"Who wants coffee?"

"I'll take a cup, Cora," Jeanette replied. As Cora brought the coffee, Jeanette said to Stephen, "Let's walk over to Britt's place and see what's going on."

The sun was just going down and the sky to the west was bright orange. Fast moving grey clouds hugged the horizon. The wind was picking up and a cold breeze was blowing fog in from the lake. They walked hand in hand down the narrow path that meandered through the wooded area that connected the mansion to Britt's place.

Jeanette approached the back door and rang the bell. From inside the house, Stephen could hear the muffled sounds of the door bell as it chimed three times. Jeanette pushed the button again. Three more chimes and then silence.

"Could she have gone somewhere?" Stephen asked. "Maybe she drove into town?"

"I don't think so. Britt doesn't drive. She lost her license a few years ago and has never shown any interest in getting it back."

Stephen could see that Jeanette was worried. She tried the door bell again. There was no activity from the house. Jeanette knocked on the door.

Jeanette said, "Let's walk around and check the windows."

The first window they came to was the kitchen. Both Stephen and Jeanette peered inside.

"Looks fine to me," Stephen said, somewhat relieved. They walked to the next set of windows. Stephen looked in and froze.

"What is it?" Jeanette asked.

"I see legs lying on a bed and it looks like there's blood. Do you have a key, Jeanette?"

"I don't. Only Britt and your uncle have a key."

Jeanette pounded on the window and called, "Britt, Britt, Britt!" She turned to Stephen, her face was white, "She's not moving, Stephen. We have to call the police."

They turned and ran back to the mansion. Jeanette threw open the back door and ran for the phone in the kitchen. Cora jumped up from the table. Bobby was sitting with a cup of coffee.

"What's going on?" he asked.

"We're calling the police. Something's happened to Britt. She's lying in her bed and not moving. We can't get in because her place is all locked up."

Bobby started for the door. "I'll break in."

Stephen grabbed his arm. "I don't think we should do that. It looks like we may be dealing with a crime scene."

Bobby pulled his arm free and shot Stephen a look.

"Crime scene? What the hell are you talking about? I'm the guard around here. I need to see what's going on. This is my responsibility."

Bobby bolted for the door as Jeanette reached someone at the sheriff's office.

"Please send help to Cliffside Manor on Pine Ridge Road. We need the police and an ambulance."

It took the police eighteen minutes to get to the mansion. By that time Bobby had broken a window in the back of Britt's house, climbed in and had confirmed that she was dead in the bedroom. There was lots of blood. Bobby was standing in the front door when the police arrived.

Once the officers saw the condition of Britt's body, they were not pleased Bobby had broken in. Bobby was ushered out of the house, crime scene tape was being unrolled, and the Michigan State Police Investigation team was called, along with the county coroner.

Stephen and Jeanette sat silently in the trophy room. Bobby had poured a drink and was pacing aback and forth. The police were not talking, but they were asking questions.

"Ms. St. Jacques, I'm Detective Drew and this is Detective Franklin. We have a few questions we would like to ask of Mr. Kahle. Would it be possible to talk to him?"

Jeanette was holding on to Stephen, quietly crying into his shoulder. She looked up at the detective.

"I'm sorry, Mr. Kahle's in California. Once we reach him with this terrible news, I'm sure he will be returning as soon as possible. Can you give us any more details? Was it a suicide? Was it...," Jeanette paused. "When I break the news to Mr. Kahle, I have to tell him something."

"As you know, Ms. St. Jacques, these things take time. Once our technicians go over the scene, we will all have a lot more information. Could you tell us who discovered Ms. Adolfson?"

Jeanette explained to Detective Drew that Britt had not been seen all day. Detective Franklin interrupted and asked Stephen if he could step away. He had a few questions of his own to ask.

Detective Drew asked Jeanette if there was a private area where they could call Mr. Kahle. She got up and led the detective to her office. Jeanette didn't know how to break the news to Phillip. She sat quietly for a moment at her desk before picking up the phone. She dialed Phillip's hotel and asked to speak to Mr. Kahle. The phone rang twice and Phillip answered.

"Oh, Phillip," Jeanette started crying.

"What's wrong?"

"I don't know how to tell you this, but Britt, Britt's dead."

There was a long silence on the phone.

"Jeanette, was there an accident?"

"We're not quite sure, but the police are here now and there is a detective with me in my office. Yes, I'll put him on." Jeanette handed the phone to Detective Drew.

Chapter 28

Moon's back was killing him. He rolled over on his side. Why was he on the floor? He heard snoring from across the room. It all came back. Oh yeah, Paulie was staying at his place.

Moon remembered coming back to the apartment with two six-packs and three bottles of wine. He thought about how mad he got when Paulie refused to drink the wine he bought. What an ass, Moon thought. Since when was Manischewitz Black Berry cheap wine?

Moon sat up and stretched. Once Paulie started drinking beer last night, the stories really flowed. Even though Moon had drunk plenty, it wasn't enough to block out Paulie's stories. Even if only half of them were true, Moon knew he was dealing with a dangerous man.

The phone rang, piercing the stillness of the morning. Moon jumped up and stumbled to the phone. He tried to grab it before it rang again, waking up his guest. It was Jimmy Hebbard, a fellow picketer from Mr. Kahle's mansion.

"Hey, Jimmy," Moon whispered into the phone. "What's going on."

"Don't bother picketing today or any other day, for that matter. A bunch of us just got grilled by the cops. I think old man Kahle's girlfriend is dead and nobody knows what's happened."

"Dead?" Moon glanced over at Paulie, sleeping on the couch.

"Yeah, can you believe it? They were asking us a bunch of questions, like they think one of us had something to do with it. I don't know what happened, but it doesn't look good. I'm just telling you to not come down for your schedule today. I'd lay very low if I was you, with your record and everything."

"Shit, Jimmy. This sounds bad. Give me a call if you get any more information, will you?" Moon put down the phone. He glanced over at Paulie again.

Moon grabbed a towel and washcloth and headed down to the communal bathroom. When he returned, Paulie was sitting at the card table, looking out the dusty window.

"Morning," Moon said warily.

"What's good about it?" Paulie barked.

"Ah, well, for starters I said morning, not good morning," Moon replied. "Paulie, were you here all night or did you slip out and go somewhere?"

"After all those cheap beers you bought, I flopped on the couch and fell asleep. Why?"

"That call I just got. It was from a guy that pickets the Kahle place with me. Looks like something happened to Kahle's girlfriend. She's dead and the cops are asking a lot of questions."

Paulie stood up. "No shit. And you think I did it?"

"That ain't what I said. Nobody knows what happened. People don't get bumped off much around here so I think the heat's gonna to be turned way up until this thing gets figured out. If you had anything to do with this, I need to know, is all."

"You're nuts. You're spending too much time with them dead birds. I don't even know who this Kahle guy is, I never heard of his girlfriend and besides that gate, I've never been close to the place."

Moon paced back and forth. "It doesn't matter. It's going to make snatching Stephen a lot harder with all this attention. With this shit going on, I don't like this deal much anymore. You need to get the hell out of here fast."

Paulie's face darkened. He stomped over to Moon.

"Sorry, buddy. That ain't happening. I came up here to do a job and I'm sure as hell going to do it."

Moon looked up at Paulie.

"Paulie, think about this for a minute. Probably where you're from, kidnappings and mysterious deaths go on all the time. It ain't like that here.

The cops know Stephen was already grabbed and got away. Now some dumb blond is dead at the same place Stephen is staying. This doesn't sound much like a coincidence to me. The cops are going to be crawling around here like ants at a picnic. I already spent my time in lockup. I don't want to go back. So if I was you, I'd grab your suitcase and hit the road while you can."

Paulie reached down and jerked Moon up by his pajama top. Moon's feet were swinging in the air. One slipper fell to the floor with a plop.

"Well, that ain't quite like I got it figured, you little weasel. You told me you had a plan and you better carry it out. I need that kid, and guess what? I'm not leaving without him. I'll be a nice guy and kick in some extra dough. I'll give you five hundred but you need a plan to get me out of here with what I came for. If you don't, the cops will be wondering what happened to you, too. You got that, Moonie?"

Moon's feet were flailing in the air and his face was turning red. His pajama top was knotted so tight against his chest he could only nod in agreement. Paulie let go and Moon hit the floor with a thud. He lay on the floor gasping for breath.

Chapter 29

Phillip caught a red eye to Chicago and then got a small commuter plane to Green Bay, where he rented a car and drove back to Grand View. While in Los Angeles, he had contacted Britt's family in Sweden and together, they made the necessary arrangements.

Detective Drew had commandeered the trophy room as his working area. He had questioned Cora, Bobby, Stephen, and Jeanette several times, each time asking slightly different questions. He still wasn't giving out any meaningful information. Jeanette was surprised when the police marched several picketers into the trophy room to meet with the Detectives.

Jeanette was trying to get some things accomplished in her office, but it just wasn't happening. She could not concentrate and whenever she thought about Britt or Phillip, she would break down in tears. The mansion had always been a respite from the real world. It was a safe place where good things always seemed to happen. Oh, there were arguments and hurt feelings now and then, but they never seemed to last.

Detective Drew stuck his head in her door.

"Jeanette, could I please have a moment of your time?"

"Certainly." Jeanette dabbed her red eyes with a tissue.

The detective entered her office, closed the door behind him and pulled up a chair next to Jeanette's desk.

"As you know, I've been talking to everyone who either was around or could have been around at the time of Ms. Adolfson death. I understand there was a small party the night before Ms. Adolfson died and towards the end, she and Mr. Kahle had words. He wanted her to leave the gathering and she didn't want to. Is that correct?"

"I wouldn't call it 'words'. I know Mr. Kahle wanted to leave because he had to get up early for his trip to California and he asked Britt to leave with him, but she wanted to stay with the party. That's really all that happened."

Detective Drew scribbled a few notes. "I understand Mr. Kahle's nephew was also at the gathering."

"Yes, he was, and so was I."

"Did it seem to you that Ms. Adolfson had an interest in staying at the party to be with Mr. Kahle's nephew?"

"Britt was a flirt. What more can I say. She loved to flirt and she seemed to enjoy being the center of attention, especially in front of Mr. Kahle. But, as far as I know, that's as far as it went. It was a game for her. She's been a flirt for all the years I've known her. This was certainly not an isolated incident the night of the party. And I've seen no signs that Stephen was romantically interested in Ms. Adolfson."

"I see." Detective Drew scribbled some more. "But it can be said that when Mr. Kahle left the party, he was angry with Ms. Adolfson, is that right?"

"Well, yes, probably a little perturbed. She knew how to push his buttons, if you will. But certainly not angry enough to do anything, if that's what you're implying."

Detective Drew did not comment. He just continued writing in his notepad.

As he drove down Pine Ridge Road to the main gate, Phillip noticed there were no picketers around. When he pulled into the circular driveway, he saw several strange cars parked along the drive, along with one police car. Phillip was lifting his suitcases from the trunk of the rental car as Detective Drew approached him.

"Mr. Kahle, I'm Detective Drew. I'm so sorry to hear about your tragic news. When you get settled in, I would like to ask you a few questions. If you don't mind, I've set myself up in your trophy room."

"Thank you for your kind words. No, I don't mind a bit. Please give me a few minutes to put my things away."

Twenty minutes later, Phillip sat down next to Detective Drew.

Chapter 30

Moon was crumpled on the floor in a heap. After several minutes, he caught his breath. He got up on one knee and grabbed the table for support before pulling himself to a shaky standing position.

"Okay, Paulie. I get five hundred and you get out of Grand View with the damn kid. You go back to New York and this whole business is over. It's a deal, but this has to happen fast. You stay here and I'll get this thing started. With what's just happened at Kahle's we don't have time to argue or screw around."

Paulie didn't say a word. He just stood and stared at Moon. Paulie was used to being in charge. He didn't like being talked to like this but he was smart enough to know he probably did need some help at this stage of the game, at least for now.

"I need to get out of here and find out what happened over there. I'm gonna talk to some of the guys who were picketing when all this shit happened. Then I can figure out how we can grab the kid. Believe me, I want this to work more than you do."

Paulie smiled, "You better get it right, is all I'm going to say."

Moon grabbed a jacket and headed out. Paulie heard him scramble down the stairs and slam the front door. He sat in Moon's overstuffed chair and stared out the window for about twenty minutes, enjoying his time alone. His head hurt a little from all those cheap beers the night before.

A TV game show was playing from a room down the hall. He heard the next door neighbor walk out and close the door. Paulie could hear the sound of fumbling keys, the door locking and what appeared to be manly footsteps echo down the hallway and start down the steps.

Paulie watched out the window as an elderly, bald man exited the building. The man was old, but big. He had on a flannel shirt, jeans and some tan boots. He was dressed like everyone else in this God-forsaken part of the country. Paulie glanced down at his suit.

Shit! He thought said to himself. No wonder I'm standing out like a sore thumb.

Paulie walked over to Moon's closet. He shrugged off his suit coat and grabbed one of Moon's flannel shirts. He put one arm through the sleeve. The shirt was way too small. Paulie tossed it back into the closet and walked over to the door. He inched the door open and looked down the hallway. The game show was sounding louder, but he didn't see any activity.

Paulie walked over to the old man's room and tried the door. It was locked. He reached into his pants and removed a credit card from his wallet. In a few seconds the door swung open. Paulie stepped inside and closed the door.

The old man kept a neat apartment. No dirty dishes in the sink, no piles of clothes in the corners, and no bird carcasses lying on tables. Too bad I'm not hiding out over here, Paulie thought.

Paulie walked into the bedroom. He picked up a photograph on the nightstand next to the bed. It was a picture of the old man, looking about twenty years younger. He was standing with a woman who must have been his wife. Two little girls were standing in front of them. Paulie set the picture down and checked the nightstand drawer for a gun. The drawer contained a bible, a deck of cards and some loose change.

He walked over and opened the closet. He picked out two flannel shirts and a pair of pants. He looked around to see what else he may need. Shoes. Paulie reached down and grabbed a pair of work boots.

He noticed a rifle standing in the far corner of the closet. Paulie picked it up. It was a beauty. It was a lever action Winchester 30-30. Paulie thought it may come in handy. Especially if he had to be out in the woods again. This was a rifle that could take out a bear. He grabbed the rifle and rearranged some hangers to make sure the closet looked exactly like it did before he came in. He walked back and stopped at the door to listen.

Paulie slipped open the door and peaked out. He put one foot out and halted. Someone was coming up the stairs. Paulie darted back into the apartment and softly closed the door. His heart was racing. He stood in back of the door, ready to smash anyone entering the room with the rifle butt. The steps got closer. Paulie's muscles tightened as footsteps approached the door. He heard a key go into the lock. Paulie readied the rifle. The door swung open. Paulie held his breath and brought the rifle back to swing.

"Mr. Durand?" a woman's voice called from the bottom of the stairs. "Would you be kind enough to come down and look at my kitchen drain? It seems to be backing up again, and I know how good you fixed it last time."

"Certainly, Bea. Let's give it a look." The door swung shut and the old man descended back down the stairs. Paulie relaxed. He waited a minute and then ducked back into Moon's apartment, locking the door behind him.

Paulie tried on his new wardrobe. He slid into the shirt just fine but he had trouble zipping up the pants. Just a little too small. He pushed his feet into the boots. They were very tight. He winced and hoped they would loosen up with a little wear. He walked over to a mirror Moon had in the kitchen. Much better, Paulie thought.

Chapter 31

Moon sat in a Café in Munising with Jerry and Karen, two fellow picketers. The café was at the end of Maple Street, perched on the edge of a bluff overlooking the harbor. They were all drinking black coffee and smoking cigarettes.

"There goes another one," Jerry said, pointing to a ferry just leaving the harbor.

"That's the business we should be in," Karen replied. "We've only been here for about half an hour and that's the third boat we've seen headed towards Pictured Rocks."

"It's the season," Moon chimed in. "You better do it while you can. Once October hits, it's all over."

Jerry said, "Speaking of 'it's all over', I guess our picketing days are done for good. That was a good gig while it lasted. It's so damn hard to make any money around here."

Moon sighed and took a sip of coffee. "So, you were both at the mansion when the cops came. What happened to Mr. Kahle's girlfriend?"

Jerry was the first to respond, "We're not sure. All of a sudden, two police cars raced up, then an ambulance. The guard had opened up the gate a few minutes before and they all tore into the driveway. We tried to sneak in, but one cop was guarding the entrance, so we could only listen from the gate."

"I think she killed herself," Karen said.

Moon looked puzzled, "Why would she do that? She lived in a mansion, had all the money she needed, and she didn't have to work. She had it made."

"I don't think so either, Karen," Jerry said.

Karen thought for a moment. "You know, money isn't everything. Who knows what demons she had running around in her head? If she didn't kill herself, she either died of natural causes or she was murdered. I'm not exactly sure how old she was, but I don't think it's likely she died of natural causes."

Jerry added, "Maybe it was drugs?"

Moon said, "Yeah, maybe. But I thought she was some kind of health nut. From what they say, she didn't even eat meat."

Jerry asked, "Do you really think she could have been murdered?"

"Who could have done it?" Moon asked. "Mr. Kahle? The nephew?" He paused, "An intruder?"

Jerry replied, "I heard that someone was after Mr. Kahle's nephew. Maybe it was them?"

Moon set down his cup of coffee. He wanted to steady his shaking hand.

"Yeah, maybe," Moon whispered.

"Come on, Jerry, let's go." Karen stood up. "We're headed over to the movies to see 'The Stepford Wives'. Want to come with us?"

Moon threw a dollar on the table. "No, I got to go. If you find out anything more about what happened, let me know."

During the drive back to Grand View from Munising, Moon wondered if Stephen was thinking about the same thing he was. Who killed Kahle's girlfriend? Was it related to Stephen's kidnapping?

A smile broke out on Moon's face. This was the answer to his problem. Now he had a plan to get Stephen back into the clutches of Paulie and to get both of them out of his life and make some damn good money for himself on top of it.

Chapter 32

Jeanette had retreated to her room. She was exhausted. The shock of Britt's death together with the relentless questions from the police had worn her out. It was so sad to watch Phillip deal with his grief. She got the feeling that the authorities seemed to think one of them was responsible for Britt's death. It was all too much to deal with. She knew Stephen and Phillip were feeling overwhelmed as well. The serenity of Cliffside Manor was shattered. She wondered if it would ever return.

There was a soft knock on her door. She opened it and saw Stephen standing there with a forlorn look on his face.

Stephen said, "Hi, sorry to bother you. I just needed someone to talk to."

"I'm glad you came by, I was just sitting here being miserable by myself. Let's grab a cup of coffee and head up to the library."

Once in the library, Stephen stood at the window and gazed down at the pounding surf.

"My mind's been racing and I just wanted to see what you thought about some questions I have," Stephen started. "We know Britt's dead, but I can't figure out why the police won't tell us anything. Was it a suicide? Was it something else?"

"I've been wondering the same thing," Jeanette replied. "But think about it, Stephen. If it was a suicide, there would be no questions. Wouldn't they just come out and tell us that Britt had killed herself and ask us why we thought it happened?"

"Yes, unfortunately, that's what I've been thinking too. And that's why it seems at times like they think one of us did it!"

Jeanette said, "Well, if it was murder, someone had to do it."

Stephen nodded. "That's the scary part. I know you didn't do it, I didn't do it, and Uncle Phillip didn't do it. So who's left?"

Jeanette thought. "You're forgetting one very important thing. You were kidnapped just days ago. It seems to me these two things must be related."

"But I was being held as an insurance policy on a gambling debt my father owed. Britt and Uncle Philip didn't have anything to do with that. Why would someone take my father's problems out on Britt?"

"Stephen, you're attempting to apply logic to criminal activity. Who knows how those people think?"

Stephen turned from the window.

"Let's try and think of another angle. What about those protesters at the gate every day. That's not a normal thing. We know Britt was hated by all of the hunting organizations around here."

"They never caused trouble before," Jeanette said.

"But they hated Britt. Maybe one of the picketers broke in and killed her?"

"At first they all seemed to be local people, people I knew. Lately, I saw some strangers were picketing, too."

"We also know she was a flirt," Stephen said. "Maybe one of her old boyfriends came back for revenge? We don't really know her past, do we? What went on in Hollywood? Maybe there's a reason she never wanted to go back?"

Jeanette took a sip of her coffee. "Hmm, I never thought of that. Maybe Britt was really just hiding out up here in the north woods."

Stephen got up from the chair. "My head's aching from constantly thinking about this. I'd like to go to the theater and get lost in a movie, what do you think?"

"That's a great idea!" Jeanette responded.

They walked out of the library down the hall to the theater room. Built-in shelves from floor to ceiling held hundreds of movie reels. Stephen read the titles as he went from shelf to shelf.

Stephen said, "I think it would be fitting to watch one of Uncle Philip's movies."

"How about 'Attack of the Piltdown Man'?" Jeanette asked. "The movie that built this house."

"Perfect, let me see if I can find it."

After a few minutes of searching, Stephen opened the first canister and threaded the film into the projector. They settled into two red velvet theater seats and started watching the movie.

As the opening credits appeared on the screen, Stephen whispered to Jeanette, "Look, the creepy old mansion in the movie looks just like this house."

"I know. Remember, I told you, your uncle built this house as a tribute to this movie."

In the darkness, Stephen wanted to reach over and take Jeanette's hand.

After the movie, Stephen returned the reels to their metal cases and put them back on the shelf. He and Jeanette returned to the library.

"How did you like it?" Jeanette asked.

"I thought it was great. A little campy, for sure, but I felt the whole movie took place right here, not on some movie lot. The front of the house looked the same. The foyer was identical. The big stairway leading to the second floor was the same. Even the library, where the scientist gets killed, looked exactly like this room."

"I've seen the movie a few times myself," Jeanette said. "It's hard to believe that they made it on a set and not right here at Cliff-side Manor."

Stephen got up and walked over to a large world globe sitting on an antique wrought iron stand.

"This has to be the same one used in the movie," Stephen said, spinning the dark brown globe. "And look, this lions head on the wall. It looks just like the one the mad scientist turned to open the secret passageway to his laboratory."

Stephen grabbed the lion head and twisted it. He heard a soft click as the bookcase in front of him silently swung open.

Jeanette jumped up, "What did you do?"

"Nothing! I just turned this, just like in the movie and the bookcase swung open!"

Stephen and Jeanette peered into the pitch black opening behind the bookcase.

Chapter 33

Moon drummed his fingers on the bar at the Freighter View. A half-full glass of beer was in front of him. He was nervous. He knew five hundred bucks was riding on his next move and he didn't want to blow it. He picked up his glass and thought to himself, I'll make the call after one more beer. Moon waved to the bartender.

"Frankie, get me another draft, will you?"

"Okay, Moonie. Here you are. Something bothering you today?"

"No, why?"

"You seem kind of quiet. You know, most of the time when you're in here, I can't shut you up. But today, not a word."

Moon sipped the foam off his beer.

"I just got a few things on my mind, that's all."

"Okay, just checking," the bartender said, turning to attend to another customer at the end of the bar.

Moon walked over to the public phone. The booth was constructed to look like an antique phone booth from a London pub. Moon entered the booth, a light switched on as the door closed.

Moon cleared his throat a few times and said a few practice words using a disguised voice, which sounded much lower. He pulled a piece of paper from his pocket and dialed. The phone rang four times and then switched over to an answering machine. Moon heard Jeanette's voice on the recorded message, "Thank you for calling the office of Phillip Kahle Productions. Mr. Kahle is not available to take your call. At the sound of the tone, please leave your name, number and the nature of your call."

Moon heard the beep. In his disguised voice, Moon said, "This message is for Jeanette. I got some news you may want to know about who grabbed Kahle's nephew. I also got some info about what happened to Kahle's girlfriend, there. You need to bring five hundred bucks to Devil's Kitchen Cave at nine tomorrow night. Only you and that nephew, no one else. I get the money, you get names."

Moon stuffed his paper back into his pocket and hung up the phone. He walked back over to the bar. He was drenched with sweat.

Frankie was bent over washing bar glasses and glanced up as Moon climbed back onto his bar stool.

"You look like shit, Moon. You got the flu?"

Chapter 34

Stephen was staring into the dark entrance of the passageway. He turned to Jeanette, "Is this another part of the movie? Does this go anywhere or is it just a joke Uncle Phillip had installed?"

Jeanette peered into the opening. "I don't know, Stephen. I never knew this was here. Your Uncle never mentioned it and I never saw anyone use it."

"Come on, let's see where it goes," Stephen said.

"Let me get a flashlight," Jeanette said. "I'm not walking into that darkness without any light."

"There must be lights somewhere," Stephen said, feeling around the edge of the door. "Yes, here's a switch."

Stephen flipped the switch and a string of dim, dusty bulbs turned on, illuminating the passageway.

Slowly Stephen and Jeanette entered the opening. The air was cool and smelled musty. As they inched along, they could see the corridor had been used as a storage place for hundreds of props from Phillip's many movies.

They passed a suit of arms, a guillotine, and a huge stack of bundled movie posters leaning in the corner. Stephen ducked under a giant model airplane hanging from the ceiling.

Stephen turned to Jeanette, "I wonder if this goes anywhere, or is it just an elaborate storage area for old movie junk?"

They turned a corner and Jeanette let out a scream. Just ahead of them in the gloom was an enormous stuffed bear, its arms thrust upwards in a menacing way.

Jeanette started laughing, "I feel like I'm in one of Phillip's old horror movies myself. I forgot all about this bear. Phillip used to place it out on the patio when we had parties for his Hollywood friends. It opens in the back and that's were your uncle kept bottles of expensive whisky."

"I never heard of a bear bar," Stephen laughed.

"Britt hated that bear. She thought it was cruel to use a dead animal as a party prop. She made him get rid of it, but I see it's still around."

Twenty feet past the bear the corridor ended and they looked down a narrow set of stairs.

"I guess this answers your question, Stephen. It must go somewhere."

They followed the staircase down to a landing and continued walking along a tunnel that ended in front of a large wooden door.

"So where do you think this goes?" Stephen asked.

"I can't imagine. I'm so turned around down here, I'm not sure what direction we're headed. I guess we need to open it and find out."

Stephen twisted the door knob. The heavy door slowly swung open with a loud creak.

"Those hinges need some oil," Jeanette exclaimed, holding her ears.

"It looks like we're in a basement," Stephen muttered, with a hint of disappointment in his voice. "Are we under the garage?"

"I don't think so. I never saw a basement in the garage, but then again, I never knew there was a secret passageway from the library either!" Jeanette said.

The basement was also used as a storage area, but the items seemed to be more like household things, not movie props. At the end of the cellar was another stairway, this time leading up.

Stephen turned to Jeanette, "I guess we'll find out where this goes now."

They climbed the stairway. Stephen turned the door handle and pushed. Part of a wall swung open and they entered into a living room area. Stephen turned around to see the opening was once again, part of a floor to ceiling bookcase.

Jeanette gasped, "I don't believe this! We're in Britt's house!"

"We probably shouldn't be over here," Stephen said. "It's still closed off and considered a crime scene."

"I know," Jeanette replied. "But I want to see something."

She walked over to the bedroom and glanced in. Jeanette covered her face and shuttered.

"Oh, Stephen, this is terrible. We have to leave."

Stephen followed her and looked in. The room looked the same as when they had peeked through the window and found Britt. Except now they could see a lot more of the surroundings. Lamps were broken on the floor and bedding was tossed around. There was a large stain of blood on the bed. It looked like a terrible struggle had taken place.

"I think this answers our questions, Jeanette. This was no suicide. Let's get out of here."

They headed back to the basement and climbed the stairs back to the passageway in silence. Stephen quietly took Jeanette's hand in his as they walked down the corridor. They were both thinking what the ramifications of this discovery could mean. They reached the turn in the corridor and walked towards the stuffed bear when Stephen suddenly stopped.

"What's wrong?" Jeanette asked.

“Look!” Stephen said, pointing to the floor behind the bear.

“What is it?” Jeanette asked.

Stephen bent down, pulled a handkerchief out of his back pocket and slowly picked up a bloody knife by the tip.

“It’s my knife. It’s the knife Uncle Phillip gave me.”

Jeanette stared. “Stephen, it’s the murder weapon.”

“I know.”

Chapter 35

Paulie was sitting on a chair looking outside the front window. It was five in the afternoon and he was getting stir crazy sitting around Moon's filthy room. Every now and then a car would drive by. Paulie stretched, got up and grabbed a beer from the fridge. As he walked by the card table, he tried not to look at the disgusting bird, turned inside out. Paulie returned to the chair and glanced at his watch. He spotted some movement out the window and observed a car pulling up to the curb.

A man, who appeared to be in his early forties got out, walked over to the passenger side and held the door open as a bleached blonde got out. She was carrying a six pack. Paulie stood up. Paulie thought the blonde was a little big, but he had to admit, she was built. Her blouse was half unbuttoned and pulled out of her jeans on one side.

Paulie watched as they entered the building. He could hear them climb the stairs. They walked passed Moon's room and stopped next door. The woman was laughing as the man fumbled for his keys.

"Come on Lester, I don't have all day. My old man's going to be home in a few."

The door opened and slammed close. A few minutes later, Paulie heard the deep thump of bass reverberating through the wall from a stereo next door. He could hear muffled laughter coming from the other room and then sounds like furniture being moved. After several more minutes the pounding bass was replaced by another noise, the unmistakable sound of a couple making love.

Paulie paced the floor and finished his beer. The moans and thumps from next door were driving him crazy. He started thinking about Annette from Queens. He had met her at an Italian bakery where he was shaking down the owner for protection money. Annette was built similar to the blonde next door. She was about the same height but not so big in the hips. They had been seeing each other for about eight months.

Paulie slammed down his empty beer bottle. He had to get out of Moon's disgusting room. He couldn't sit and listen to what was going on next door for another moment.

Paulie rummaged through his suitcase and pulled out his traveling butterfly net. He walked down the stairs and headed to the back of the rooming house. The backyard backed up to a wooded area. He peeked around the building to make sure nobody could spot him from the road.

Paulie walked to the edge of the forest. He peered into the woods searching for butterflies. After a few minutes, he spotted a beautiful dark blue skipper. Paulie ran after the specimen, his net swooping in the air. Back and forth he went, always inches from his quarry.

Paulie stumbled and fell to his knees. Those damn boots he had stolen were pinching his feet. He watched as the blue butterfly disappeared back into the woods.

Paulie got up and walked back and forth along the edge of the forest for twenty more minutes, searching for more butterflies. He gave a half-hearted chase after a big, bright yellow one, only to have it flitter back into the woods. That was enough. He gave up in disgust. His feet were hurting. He returned to Moon's room and stashed his net away.

Paulie thought about The Freighter View Tavern. A cold beer and some company sounded very inviting. It was a much better idea than sitting around this stinking room.

The rooming house was on 10th street. He figured it should only be about a few blocks to the bar. Paulie slipped out of the room and closed the door softly behind him, making sure the lock was not set.

As he walked down the sidewalk to the bar, he watched to make sure no one was following him. After walking three blocks, the work boots started hurting his feet. He reached down and untied the laces, hoping that would give him some relief. By the time Paulie made it to the bar, he was limping badly from blisters on both feet.

A tour bus was parked in front. 'Grand Rapids Lake Circle Tours' was painted in big white letters on the side. Paulie had never seen the Freighter so crowded. The place was packed. Quite a few tourists were sitting at tables having lunch. Other people were standing at the bar having drinks.

Paulie scanned the room. He saw a lot of older people, probably from the bus. There were a few guys who looked like locals and then his gaze stopped at a table in the corner where two younger women were sitting. They weren't dressed like tourists. One girl, the blonde, was wearing a mini-skirt. The other girl, a red head, was wearing a tight sweater with a plunging neckline. Paulie limped over to their table, pulled out a chair and sat down.

The girls stopped talking and turned towards their intruder.

"Sorry, mister, this table's taken," the blonde said.

"Yeah, I noticed," Paulie replied. "It's packed in here and my feet are killing me."

A waitress walked by and Paulie tugged at her sleeve. "Get these ladies another drink and I'll have a whiskey and water."

The red head was about to tell Paulie to go find another seat, but the prospect of a free drink made her change her mind. Instead, she said, "Where you from, big guy? It don't sound like you're from around here?"

Not wanting to give out too much information, Paulie replied, "I'm from the east coast, up near Boston. What about you girls? You don't exactly fit in with these tourists, either."

"We're dancers. Exotic dancers,"The blonde said.

"We were exotic dancers," the red head corrected. "Now we're just unemployed."

"What happened?" Paulie asked.

The blonde said, "We were dancing for some creep who owns a club in Munising and, let's just say, he was more interested in taking our earnings out in trade than in our dance routines, and that don't fly with me, honey. I'm not a prude or nothing like that, but first you gotta show me some cash before we can discuss other matters, you know?"

The red head lit a cigarette. "We got expenses. Our costumes, our shoes, don't even get me started. Roxanne, here," she nodded at the blonde, "had this great idea to get us out of Grayling and thought we could make some money dancing. I wanted to go to Lansing, but no, she knew this guy in Munising."

Roxanne interrupted, "I didn't know he was such a jerk, Lisa. It's not my fault."

Lisa, the red head, continued, "Now we're staying in a campground and we don't even have enough money for gas to get us back home."

"Don't worry about that," Paulie said. "If you girls want to do a little partying, I'll make it worth your while." He pulled a fifty dollar bill out of his wallet and slammed it on the table.

"Hey, Paulie. What's going on?"

Paulie turned to see Moon standing next to the table. Moon looked like he was about to fly into a rage.

"What the hell is this?" Moon yelled, his face bright red. "You're supposed to be laying low in the room, remember? Didn't you see those two cops walk through here half an hour ago?"

"Shut up," Paulie said as he jumped to his feet. He got up so quickly his chair flipped over and hit the floor with a bang. Moon and Paulie stood glaring at each other. The whole place became quiet as everyone turned to watch.

Paulie turned to the girls, "Come on, let's get out of here."

Moon stood there. "What? Are you crazy? Where're you taking them?"

"To your little love nest, Moon Pie. I think it's about time you have a little fun, buddy. Looks like you're about to explode."

Moon picked up the fallen chair, slid it back under the table and followed Paulie and the girls out to their car. Paulie and Moon climbed in the back seat.

During the short drive back to his place, Moon quietly told Paulie about his call to Jeanette and how they were all set up to meet Stephen at a place called Devil's Kitchen Cave.

When they got back to Moon's place, they had a few beers. The girls earned their gas money, checked out of the campground and headed over the Mackinac Bridge back to Lower Michigan.

Chapter 36

Stephen looked at the stunned expression on Jeanette's face and knew exactly what she was thinking.

"Jeanette, I didn't do this."

"I know that, but how on earth did your knife get here?"

"I don't know. It's always been in my bedroom, in the top drawer of the bureau."

"Stephen, we won't be the only ones asking these questions."

"I guess we need to find an answer. Since this is evidence, I'm going to put it back where we found it. We have to get the authorities. Jeanette, I hate to say this, but finding that knife makes me feel the person who did this is a lot closer to the house than some stranger from the outside, like one of those demonstrators."

Jeanette did not respond. When they returned to the back of the hidden bookcase in the library, Stephen worked the mechanism and the bookcase quietly slid open. Jeanette felt relieved to be in the familiar and safe setting of the library again.

"Stephen, let's go to my place and try and make some sense out of all this."

"Good idea."

As they passed his room, Stephen said, "My door is never locked. Anyone could come in and rummage around whenever they wanted to."

Stephen sat down on the end of the couch in Jeanette's room. Jeanette said, "Relax for a moment. I'll go to the kitchen and get us both a glass of wine."

While she was gone, Stephen stood up and paced the floor.

Jeanette returned with the drinks. She put the glasses on the coffee table in front of the couch and sat down next to Stephen. He reached over and hugged her. Their lips met. All the tension and doubt from the past few days disappeared as they held each other.

"It's hard to feel happy about meeting you in the middle of this dreadful time," Jeanette whispered.

"I know. You've said exactly what I've been thinking, but I didn't know quite how to say it," Stephen replied. "You know how bad this is looking for me, don't you? I'm new to the area, Britt was coming on to me and she was causing problems for Uncle Phillip."

Jeanette shook her head. "Stephen, the more I think about it, I think it has to be one of those picketers."

Stephen continued, "Don't forget, Britt's house was locked when she was killed and now we find my knife in a secret passageway that only one or two people probably know about. This all adds up to me looking very guilty!"

Stephen buried his head into his hands. After a minute he looked up and said, "I have to go to the police with this, because if I don't, it will look even worse for me."

Jeanette held him close. "I know it looks bad, but we both know there has to be another answer. We have to work together and see what we can figure out. I'm going to get more wine, this could be a long night."

On the way back from the kitchen, Jeanette ducked into her office and grabbed a pad of paper and a pen so she and Stephen could write down some ideas.

Jeanette noticed her answering machine light was blinking. She bent down and hit the play button. She heard a vaguely familiar voice say, "I have information you may want to know."

Jeanette listened to the complete message, hit the play again button and listened to it a second time.

She ran back to her room.

"Stephen, we can't go to the police yet. I just got a message on my answering machine from someone who is claiming to know who killed Britt. He tried to disguise his voice, but I think I know who it is."

Stephen jumped up. "Who is it?

"It sounded like a guy named Moon, Moon Murchie!"

Chapter 37

As Moon was making coffee he kept thinking about what had happened the night before. This was really turning out to be a pretty good deal. Last night's party, with its side benefits, hadn't cost him a dime and after the call to Jeanette, he should be getting the big payoff he had always dreamed of. Not bad, he thought. Not so bad at all.

Moon poured a cup of coffee, walked over to Paulie and gently shook him. "Hey, get up."

Paulie groaned and tried to roll over. He was in the middle of an erotic dream, both girls from the night before were rolling around in his bed. Moon was not in the picture.

The aroma of hot coffee helped Paulie come out of it. He struggled to sit up. His legs were tangled up in an old bed sheet.

"Damn it, Moon. You'd screw up a wet dream."

"We got some planning to do. You want this to be over with, don't you? We need to make sure this comes off smooth."

Paulie took a sip of coffee and stretched. "Okay, genius, tell me what we have to do."

Moon pulled out a map. It was a detailed forest service map showing all the trails, logging roads and elevations located in the area of Devil's Kitchen Cave.

"I got it all figured out. We leave here at seven. Old lady Fitzpatrick lives on the third floor and she never locks her car. We grab her car and head over to Forest Highway 13. See, it's here on the map. It's an old logging road that runs almost to the cave."

Moon smoothed out the map and pointed. "We drive to this point and walk from here. We leave early enough so we can climb up to the cave. We'll be high enough to see anything going on around us. If anything looks funny, we take this trail here back to the car and get the hell out of there. If it's only Jeanette and the kid, like I think it will be, we grab the kid and head back to the car. You drop me off on Highway 77 where I have my bicycle stashed and head back to New York with the kid. I peddle home with a grand in my pocket."

Paulie looked up from the map. "A grand? I told you five hundred."

"That was then, my friend. When you think about it, I'm the guy that did all the planning. It took a lot of work to figure this thing out. Who do you think called Jeanette and set up the meeting and everything? Without me, you'd still be hiding in the bushes somewhere with your thumb up your ass."

Paulie jumped to his feet. "Nobody talks to me like that."

Moon didn't like the look on Paulie's face. "Take it easy. Now's not the time to get all agitated," he said, with a little less conviction in his voice.

Paulie grabbed Moon by the throat. "Well, guess what? Now I got the map and I got the plan and I don't need to give you shit."

Moon cocked his fist back and punched Paulie in the face as hard as he could. Paulie didn't move. He didn't make a sound or even react like anything had happened. The only thing that changed were his eyes. Paulie's eyes narrowed and looked cold.

Paulie took his free arm, reached over and grabbed Moon by the head. He gave a quick twist and Moon felt a snap. Moon tried to scream but all he could manage was a few soft gurgling sounds as Paulie gently lowered him to the floor.

Chapter 38

Jeanette woke up on the couch with a blanket over her. The room was dim as the first light of day illuminated the manicured grounds outside her window. She tried to move her legs. She looked down to see Stephen sleeping next to her, his legs draped over hers. An empty wine bottle was on the coffee table next to two empty glasses.

Jeanette quietly got up, hoping not to wake Stephen. She went to the kitchen, made a pot of coffee and rummaged in the pantry.

Jeanette thought about the meeting with Moon set for tonight. She wondered how he could possibly know anything. Was this his idea of a big joke? Was it worth the trouble going to meet him? She walked back to her room carrying a tray with two cups of coffee and two English muffins. Stephen was sitting on the couch, looking very tired.

"Good Morning, Stephen."

Stephen ran his fingers through his hair. "Morning, what happened last night?"

"I think we were both exhausted. I remember having a few glasses of wine and talking. Then I remember snuggling next to you after I got a blanket because we were cold. We must have fallen asleep after that."

Stephen pulled Jeanette close. "It was nice having you next to me last night."

Jeanette leaned up and kissed him. He knew she felt the same way. They held each other for a few minutes. Jeanette looked at Stephen.

"I think we need to be very careful tonight. I don't think Moon is dangerous, but I doubt he's in this alone. He has a history of following the wrong crowd, getting in trouble and paying for it. I don't want to get caught up in one of his schemes. Then again, I would want to see if he can tell us something useful."

"It does seem strange that he would have all of this information just by himself."

Jeanette nodded, "I think we should leave with enough time to get us to the cave at least an hour before the meeting. I know of a high spot above the cave where we can watch to make sure Moon is coming by himself. I've got a map of the area I can give you just in case we get separated. I've hiked all the trails back there for years, I don't need it."

"What about the money?"

"What money?" Jeanette asked.

"Didn't you say the person on phone wanted you to bring five hundred dollars?"

"If the person turns out to be Moon, like I think it will, I'll tell him Mr. Kahle would be happy to pay him a reward for Britt's killer, and it would probably be a lot more than five hundred dollars."

"What if it's someone else?" Stephen asked.

"I'll tell them the same thing," Jeanette stood up. "I need to get ready for work now. I'll probably work till around four thirty, but I'll see you at dinner. Don't mention our plans to anyone."

Stephen went to his room, showered and changed into some clean clothes. He walked around his room to see if he could find any trace of whoever may have gone in and stolen his knife. Everything seemed fine. He didn't see anything out of the ordinary. Stephen took his sketchpad to the library and sketched for a few hours. Around lunch time, he walked down to Jeanette's office.

"Do you want to have some lunch, Jeanette?"

"Yes, let me get Phillip and he can join us."

Phillip looked pale and hardly said a word. When lunch was over, Phillip walked to the door and said that he would be in his quarters for the rest of the day and to go ahead and have dinner without him.

Jeanette returned to her office and Stephen spent the afternoon walking the grounds, trying to see if he could discover any evidence of an intruder.

After dinner, Stephen met Jeanette in her room to review the final preparations for the hike to Devil's Kitchen Cave.

"We both have a flashlight and you have a map. We need to make sure Moon is alone, because we are talking about kidnapping and murder. We need to leave now if we want to get to the cave while it's still light. It won't be totally dark till around nine o'clock. We have a quarter moon, so we should be able to walk the trail back easily, if it's not too cloudy."

"Okay," Stephen replied, "let's get going."

Chapter 39

Paulie needed more beer and thought it was about time to check in with Al. He walked three blocks and found a payphone outside the IGA store. Paulie had replaced the stolen boots, which had been killing his feet, with the snake skin shoes he had brought with him from New York. The shoes didn't match his new jeans and plaid shirt look, but his feet felt much better. He dumped some coins into the pay phone and dialed.

"Yeah," Al answered.

"Al, its Paulie. I'm picking up the kid in about an hour and we'll be heading back to the city tonight. The plan I told you about is going good."

"No, it ain't. There's new plans, Paulie. There's been no sign of the dough. You-know-who told me you need to go to plan B. Just bring back a souvenir that shows everything's been taken care of. You do remember plan B, don't you?"

"Yeah, Al. Plan B's where I should whack the ki.."

"Shut up, you ass-hole!" Al screamed into the receiver. "You're talking on a phone, here. Just go to plan B like we went over before you left. Christ, Paulie, do I have to tell you everything?"

"No Al, I got it. Sorry."

"By the way, Paulie, nobody's real impressed with you so far, if you get what I mean. This better go off without a hitch or you might just wanna relocate someplace there in Michigan or wherever the hell you are for a few years. Get my drift?"

Al slammed down the phone. Paulie understood completely.

Back at Moon's room, Paulie took another look at the map Moon had provided. The route had looked a lot clearer when Moon was pointing things out. But now, Paulie thought the map had way too many lines. Some were dotted, some were in circles. The more he stared at the map, the more he was confused.

He tossed the map down and looked around Moon's room for a flashlight. He searched all the drawers in the kitchen cabinets and didn't find one. The next logical place was the closet, but it was difficult rummaging around in there because Moon, rolled up in a blanket, took up most of the space.

Finally, on top of a shelf, Paulie found one. He pushed the door to the closet closed. Paulie grabbed the rug that was on the floor in front of the kitchen sink and rolled the rifle up inside. He then put the map in his pocket, took the flashlight and headed out the door. He got to the bottom of the steps without anyone seeing him. Walking quickly through the hallway to the back of the building where the tenants parked their cars, Paulie came to a sudden stop.

"Damnit!"

Which car was Mrs. Fitzpatrick's? He peered into each car in the dirt parking area, finally spotting a car with a set of keys hanging in the ignition. Paulie put the wrapped up rifle behind the front seat. He threw the flashlight and map onto the passenger seat, got in and drove away.

About five miles out of town, he spotted what seemed to be the logging road entrance. He turned into the opening and slowly drove as the car bounced over ruts and fallen limbs. The last few miles were down an overgrown path that appeared not to have been used in the last ten years.

Finally the car reached a dead end. Paulie opened the door and hesitated. Once again, he was alone in the middle of the woods. He glanced at the map. Just as the map indicated, a narrow trail branched off to the left. Paulie took the rifle out from the rug and stood there. He looked around. There was nothing but trees. He listened as the wind blew through the leaves.

A feeling of terror was starting to grow. He flashed back to the fright he experienced the last time he found himself alone in the woods. Now, here he was, again. Maybe he should have used Moon for this part of the job and then taken care of him later.

Paulie shrugged, looked down the narrow path and started walking. His senses were on full alert. He stopped and listened to every sound coming from the surrounding woods. The trail began to climb. He hefted the rife from his right shoulder to his left. Paulie stopped. He heard voices coming from the trail above him. He dove into the woods and huddled down behind a large fallen tree.

Two women hikers strolled down the trail.

As Paulie waited for them to pass, he spotted a deep purple butterfly flitting just inches from his face. He had never seen a butterfly like this one before. He concentrated on memorizing the color patterns so he could look it up in his butterfly guidebook when he was done.

The women passed. Paulie waited a few minutes until he didn't hear any more activity. He slowly returned to the trail. Paulie started walking. He felt something crawling on his hand. He looked down to see a wood tick walking on his wrist. Paulie shook it off. He stopped and inspected his clothes. Three more ticks were on his pant leg. Paulie stopped and brushed them off. His whole body felt like bugs were crawling on him.

The trail leveled off and the woods opened up to a large, open meadow. From out of nowhere, a swarm of black flies started buzzing around his head. Paulie felt a sharp bite on his ankle. He bent down and grabbed his foot. A black fly had bitten his ankle all the way through his sock. A fly landed on his neck. He swatted it. Another landed on his other ankle and he felt a sting. Paulie shouted out as more flies descended on him. Flies were buzzing around his hands, looking for any part of him that was uncovered. Paulie stood up and started running down the path. A swarm was following him a short distance away. Paulie reached down and grabbed a handful of ferns and slapped wildly at the flies.

He ran down the trail. The meadow area merged back into the forest. Thankfully, the flies stayed back in the open area. Paulie continued walking, scratching at his bites. With the area crawling with bears, blood sucking wood ticks and biting black flies, he wondered how these people did it. The two hikers he observed seemed to actually enjoy being in the woods.

He thought of Central Park, his girlfriend Annette, the brownstones on his street, the welcoming sound of traffic, car horns and police sirens. Maybe he should just go back to the car right now. It would probably be better to take a chance of getting whacked by the boys back home, than to die by a bear or be sucked dry by something on this damned trail.

Again, the path started to climb. Paulie strained to push up the steep incline. His feet felt around for small steps in the trail that were steady enough to support him. His shoes kept slipping on the rocky, clay soil. He grabbed a tree limb and pulled on it to help him get up a steep section of the trail. Finally he reached the summit.

At the top of the hill there was a post with three wooden signs. One sign said "Lakeshore Trail" and pointed straight ahead. Another sign pointed down a path to the right said "Devils Kitchen Meadow 1/2 mile." The third sign on the post said "Devils Kitchen Cave 1/4 mile". The trail leading to the cave looked like it was headed straight up a cliff. Paulie's legs ached and his feet were killing him. He decided to head down the fairly level path to the right, the one that pointed to the meadow.

After several twists, the trail exited the woods and opened up to a beautiful field dotted with blue and white flowers. The meadow was covered with butterflies. Paulie had never seen anything like it in his life. He gazed over the field in awe. Then he saw Devil's Kitchen Cave looming up a hill right in front of him. Paulie stepped back into the cover of the woods and decided to wait and see what was going to happen next.

Chapter 40

Jeanette and Stephen walked along the Lakeshore Trail for half an hour in total silence. Jeanette had apprehensions about what was about to happen, but she didn't want to share her fears with Stephen. Jeanette was struggling with the probability that Moon could actually have any valid information to share about Britt's murder. If he did, why wouldn't he just come to Cliffside Manor and talk to them?

The only reason Jeanette could think of was Moon always had a thing for being dramatic. Maybe this was just another variation of his next big score. He was always going to do something new and different, but it never seemed to ever happen.

As Stephen walked down the trail, he was still trying to imagine how his knife could possibly have ended up in the hidden corridor behind the library. Walking through the narrow forest path made him feel uneasy. He marveled at Jeanette's fearless grace, as she moved along the trail just ahead of him. Jeanette slowed down, pointing at a faint break in the woods.

"Stephen, this is an unmarked trail that will take us to the back of Devil's Kitchen Cave."

Stephen followed Jeanette, wondering how she knew where she was going. Abruptly the trail opened up to a beautiful vista overlooking Lake Superior. The path narrowed and ran along the cliff side. Jeanette led Stephen along the trail.

"Walk slowly, Stephen. It's a long way down." Stephen didn't need to be reminded. The trail dropped down hundreds of feet to the shoreline. He pressed himself close to the side of the cliff and tried not to look down. They came to a wide spot on the trail, about fifty feet from the cave opening and stopped to catch their breath. Stephen looked out at the lake. The view was spectacular.

"Jeanette, too bad we can't stop and enjoy this view without worrying about all our problems."

As Jeanette turned to respond, a shot rang out from the meadow below. Pieces of rock exploded just above Stephen's head. Jeanette screamed, "Moon's shooting at us! Get down."

Stephen yelled, "I thought you said he wasn't dangerous?"

A rife fired again and Stephen heard the bullet zip between him and Jeanette. Jeanette lunged at Stephen to push him down. As she grabbed for Stephen, Jeanette lost her footing on the narrow ledge and disappeared over the cliff. Stephen threw himself down on the trail and attempted to work himself over to the ledge. A rifle cracked again and a bullet lodged into the path just in front of him.

Still another bullet tore past. This time, the sound came from behind. Stephen thought he must be surrounded. He inched himself to the edge of the narrow trail and frantically peered over the steep cliff for any sign of Jeanette.

Stephen turned as he heard commotion in the woods near the entrance of the trail they had just walked. Three men dressed in camouflage, each carrying an assault rife, burst from the forest. Two men ran over to Stephen and pulled him up, one on each side. A shot rang out from the meadow below. The third camouflaged man threw himself flat on the trail and started pumping bullets in the direction of the last shot.

Paulie dropped behind a rock as three bullets peppered the area around him. He jumped up, fired a round and ducked back behind a boulder. A bullet ripped though the leaves just above his head. Paulie inched out from behind the rock, searching the trail high above him for any movement.

A shot rang out and Paulie screamed in pain. He dropped his rifle and grabbed his thigh with both hands. He saw blood seeping from his leg. Paulie stumbled and fell to his knees. He tried to steady himself as he rolled down a hill.

Three more shots hit the ground just behind him. Paulie came to rest in a clump of cedar. He scrambled behind an overturned tree and pushed hard on his thigh, trying to slow the bleeding.

The men on each side of Stephen dragged him to safety behind the mouth of the cave. The man on his right loosened his grip on Stephen's arm and said, "Stephen Moorhouse, you're being arrested for the murder of Britt Adolfson."

Stephen just stood there. He was trying to comprehend what he had just heard.

"Are you kidding? What about that idiot Moon, trying to kill us?" Stephen struggled to pull away. "Let go of me. My girlfriend fell over the cliff. I need to look for her now!"

The two men restrained him.

"We have backup in the area. A team of agents have already found the shooter's car and they're headed our way. We saw Ms. St. Jacques fall and another agent is searching for her now. Please come with us, Mr. Moorhouse."

On the march back down the trail, Stephen had one agent in front of him and the other walked closely behind. Stephen's hands were handcuffed behind his back. Stephen asked the officer in front of him, "What makes you think I killed Ms. Adolfson?"

"Sir, I can't comment on the case, but I will tell you a bloody knife, identified as belonging to you, was found hidden up underneath a ceiling tile in Ms. Adolphson's bedroom."

Stephen stopped walking. The officer behind him gave him a poke.

"Get moving."

Stephen's mind was racing. Had someone moved the knife to an even more incriminating place?

Stephen walked the rest of the way in silence. He was steadily falling into a deep despair while trying to make sense of the latest developments. He found it impossible to fully comprehend what was happening. He had just been arrested for murder.

His beautiful Jeanette was probably lying dead at the base of the cliff and Moon was still roaming free.

The trail was getting dim as the moon was beginning to rise. Stephen shuffled his way down the path, following the policeman directly ahead of him. From the uneven pace, it was apparent the cops were not as familiar with the trail as Jeanette had been. Even with a bright flashlight, the agent leading the way had to stop every now and then and hunt for the trail several times before they made it back to the staging area at Cliffside Manor.

Chapter 41

Jeanette lay wedged against a fallen hickory log. Once she felt the trail crumple under her feet, she knew she was in trouble.

The cliff edge dropped straight down twelve feet but, lucky for her, a thick growth of evergreens softened her fall. She rolled another twenty feet before slamming into the side of the log.

Jeanette fought to catch her breath. She lay still as she heard more gunfire. She moved her right arm. It seemed okay. She flexed her left arm and then her legs. There didn't seem to be any broken bones. She listened for more rifle shots. She heard only silence and then in the distance she heard voices crackling over what sounded like hand-held radios. Above, she could hear men scrambling down the steep cliff face.

She slowly rolled to her knees and peered over the log into open space. She could see just beyond the log. The cliff dropped straight down to the Lake Superior shore hundreds of feet below.

There was movement above her. Two men in uniforms were headed her way. Both men had guns drawn. She knew one of them, Dave Saunders, from school. She waved her arm.

"Dave, here...over here!"

She felt the log move slightly. Both policemen stopped with a look of panic on their faces.

"Don't move, Jeanette. That log is the only thing between you and the shoreline."

The cliff was sheer where the policemen were standing and it was a very steep drop to where Jeanette lay. Dave slowly lowered himself to his hands and knees, trying not to topple over the incline. He laid flat on the ground and inched his way head first to Jeanette. Dave turned to the other policeman.

"Jim, hold my foot. I'm going to crawl closer and see if I can grab her."

The other officer held on to Dave's ankle as he inched his way closer.

"Jeanette, can you turn and grab my hand? You have to move very slowly."

Jeanette started to turn but stopped when she felt the log move closer to the cliff.

"You're close, Jeanette. My hand's only six inches away. Try again, but move slowly."

As Jeanette reached out, she felt the log give way and tumble over the edge. Jeanette pushed off with her foot and flung herself at Dave's outstretched hand. She felt strong fingers wrap around her wrist.

"Jim, hang on. I've got you, Jeanette."

Dave pulled as Jeanette slowly eased herself away from the cliff edge.

Jim was able to steady Dave as they slowly climbed back to the path up above. Once the officers pulled Jeanette to the safety of the trail, they all sat and caught their breath for several minutes.

Dave glanced over at Jeanette and saw her arm was bleeding.

"Are you okay?" Dave asked.

"My chest and arm are starting to ache," Jeanette said, rubbing her left arm.

"Let's take a look," Dave said. He pushed the sleeve of her shirt up and looked at her elbow. There was blood on her shirt. He slowly moved her forearm up and down.

"It doesn't look like it's broken. You had one heck of a fall. Lucky for you that log was there. You may have cracked a rib when you slammed into it, though."

"Let's get you back to Mr. Kahle's," Jim said. "We'll have an ambulance ready for you."

"How's Stephen? Did he get hit?"

"No, he's okay. He's headed back to Mr. Kahle's now."

Phillip was pacing back and forth on the brick driveway as Stephen and the police finally made it back to Cliffside Manor.

He had been briefed an hour earlier, when they showed up looking for his nephew. As they placed Stephen in a police car, Phillip leaned in and said, "Don't worry, Stephen. We'll get you out of this mess. This whole thing is preposterous."

"Uncle Phil, Jeanette fell off the cliff at Devil's Kitchen. She was trying to push me out of the way when someone was shooting at us. You need to find her and see if she's okay!"

Phillip turned to one of the policemen. "Is this true?"

"Yes, Mr. Kahle. We have radio contact with another team and they tell me she's been found and she's okay. A few cuts and bruises, but doing fine. They're headed back to your place now and should be here in about thirty minutes."

Phillip leaned into the police car. "Did you hear that, Stephen?"

"Yes, at least something turned out well tonight."

A policeman jumped in the driver's seat, the window next to Stephen rolled up, and the car turned down the driveway on the way to Grand View and the county jail. Stephen looked out the rear window and watched as his uncle disappeared from view.

Chapter 42

Paulie felt the ground beneath him start to get wet from his blood. He was feeling light headed. He started going over his options. He had dropped his gun and he was bleeding badly. He was immobile behind a log and he didn't know how many cops were shooting at him. He was unsure if he had made good on plan B. Was the kid still alive? If so, the boys back home were not going to be happy. He knew what that meant. Lie here and bleed to death, or try and get back home so he could get whacked. Neither option was very appealing.

Paulie winced in pain as he tried to get on his knees. He pulled himself up on the log and started hollering, "Hey, stop shooting, it's me. Here I am, hold your fire. I'm over here!"

Stephen spent a sleepless night in jail. The previous night's activities were replaying over in his mind. There were so many unanswered questions. How was Jeanette? Who had taken his knife? Why had it been moved? How could anyone possibly think he could have murdered Britt? Who had been shooting at them up at Devil's Kitchen Cave? How was Moon involved? What about that lunatic who had followed him all the way from New York and what part did he play in all of this?

Stephen finally was able to doze off sometime before dawn. He rolled over on his thin mattress as someone yelled "breakfast" and Stephen heard a tray slide into his cell. He had just finished eating a dry piece of toast and some watery oatmeal when a guard opened the cell.

"Looks like you know all the right people," the guard said, as he pushed open the cell door. "We don't get many murderers around here, and when we do, they don't get out on bond the very next day."

"I'm not a murderer," Stephen snapped.

The guard ignored him. "Your uncle's waiting for you downstairs. Don't jump bail, kid. If you do, it's going cost him half a million bucks."

Stephen said, "I'm not running away from anything. Am I free to go now?"

"Not really. But since everyone around here knows your uncle and they know he's got that security guard, you're going to be under some kind of house arrest."

Stephen followed the guard downstairs and found Uncle Phillip and Jeanette anxiously waiting for him. Jeanette rushed up to him and attempted to give him a big hug. The hug turned out to be somewhat lopsided since only one of Jeanette's arms was involved.

Stephen saw the bandage on Jeanette's left arm.

"What happened?" Stephen asked, "Did you get shot?"

"No, I scraped my elbow when I fell. Nothing serious."

Stephen and Jeanette climbed into Uncle Phillip's car and headed back to Cliffside Manor.

As they walked into the foyer, Uncle Phillip said, "Cora has prepared something for you to eat, Stephen. I imagine you're starving. It looks like you didn't get much sleep last night. Why don't you head up to your room and get some rest after lunch. We can all meet in the trophy room and update each other on all that has happened."

Stephen wolfed down his lunch and headed to his room.

Stephen heard footsteps behind him on the staircase. He turned to see Jeanette. She rushed up to him and wrapped her arms around him.

"I'm so happy you're back," she said.

Stephen hugged her close. "I thought about you all last night. Over and over I saw you fall off that cliff."

"We're both so lucky we didn't get killed," Jeanette said, hugging Stephen close. "But, we'll talk about this later. Now go upstairs and get some rest."

Stephen got to his room, took a quick shower and collapsed into bed.

Around three thirty, while Stephen was still sleeping, Detective Drew showed up at Jeanette's office looking for Mr. Kahle. Jeanette showed him into Phillip's office.

"Hello, Detective. What can I do for you? Are you here to check on Stephen?"

"No. Actually, I wanted you to know we have arrested the man who was shooting at Jeanette and your nephew last night."

Phillip jumped up. "That's great news!"

"His name is Paul De Luca. He's a small time criminal from New York City who may have some mob connections. We're still checking him out, but we think he may have followed your nephew from New York when he came to visit you."

"Stephen said he thought he may have been followed," Phillip added.

"De Luca's singing like a bird. He doesn't want to go back to New York. From what he says, Stephen's father got in a little too deep with his bookie and the mob sent him here to kidnap Stephen."

Phillip did not comment.

"We also think he was being assisted a local man by the name of Francis Murchie," the detective continued. "I sent an officer over to his house to ask him a few questions. Unfortunately, Mr. Murchie was found dead and stuffed in a closet. We've booked Mr. De Luca on suspicions of murder and kidnapping charges."

Phillip sat quietly for a few moments. "Do you think this De Luca guy could be responsible for Britt's murder, Detective?"

"The evidence does not support that theory. But it's something we will keep working on, Mr. Kahle."

Detective Drew stood, "I've taken enough of your time. I just wanted to update you in person about the man that was stalking your nephew."

Around six thirty, Stephen made an appearance in the trophy room. Jeanette and Phillip were having a drink. Jeanette ran to Stephen as he entered the room.

"How are you feeling, Stephen?" Uncle Phillip asked.

"Much better. Cora's cooking and a long nap made a big difference."

Phillip walked to the bar and handed Stephen a drink. Stephen took it and settled into an overstuffed chair. Phillip took a seat next to him.

"Detective Drew was here earlier and updated me on some developments while you slept."

Stephen turned to Uncle Phillip. "Have they found Britt's killer?"

"Unfortunately, no. It looks like you're still suspect number one. That's why I wanted us all to meet tonight. We need to put our heads together and see if we can get to the bottom of this."

Uncle Phillip proceeded to tell Stephen about Paulie De Luca and the disturbing news about the recently deceased Moon Murchie.

Stephen sat quietly. So many thoughts were running in his head. How could his father do something to put him in so much danger? He felt lucky that Paulie didn't hurt or kill him when he had the chance. And finally, he felt terrible that another person was dead.

Jeanette and Phillip sat quietly and let Stephen have his introspection. Finally Stephen looked at Jeanette and said, "I guess one mystery's solved but we still have one more to go. Now we need to figure out what happened to Britt."

Phillip was about to say something when the phone rang in Jeanette's office. She got up to answer it. Jeanette leaned out of her office doorway, "Stephen, you have a call," she said, with a slight look of irritation.

"Is it my mother?" Stephen asked.

"No"

"My dad?"

"No, it's a girl named Jill."

Stephen didn't move, he just looked at Jeanette.

"Do you want to take the call?"

Stephen thought for a moment. "I don't know."

Jeanette asked, "Should I tell her you aren't here?"

Stephen slowly rose from his chair. "No, I'll take it," he said as he entered the office. Jeanette handed him the receiver and stepped out.

Stephen settled into Jeanette's chair. "Hello."

He heard a familiar voice, "Hi, Stephen. I bet you weren't expecting to hear from me."

"You've got that right, Jill. What's going on? How did you get this number?"

"I didn't think your mother would give it to me so I had your friend Butch call and get it."

"Where are you?" Stephen asked.

"Not in Europe, if that's what your wondering."

"Why not? What happened?"

"Well, for starters, I was a real idiot. Ralph and I didn't get along and I really want to apologize for what I did to you." There was a pause. "And I'd like to see you when you get back, so I can make it up to you."

"You're right, Jill. I wasn't expecting to hear from you. I'm sorry your trip didn't work out and I appreciate your apology, but I don't think it would be a very good idea for us to get together."

"Look Stephen, I'm very sorry about what happened and I would really like to see you. How about if I take a quick trip to Michigan? I got back from Europe earlier than planned and I've never been to Michigan before. It would be fun."

Stephen thought for a moment. "No, Jill. You really hurt me when you decided to take off like you did. I've spent a lot of time thinking about what happened, thinking about us. Believe me, coming here would not be a good idea."

"But I really want to see you."

"I have to tell you, I've actually met a really fantastic girl here, and I'm hoping she'll come back with me when I go to art school."

There was a long silence on the other end of the phone. "Okay, Stephen. I'm sorry, but I can't say I'm surprised. Take care."

Stephen hung up the receiver and walked back into the trophy room.

Jeanette looked inquisitively at Stephen.

"You won't believe that call. I'll explain later."

Phillip said, "While you were on the phone, Jeanette and I were talking. Stephen, can you explain how the knife I gave you ended up hidden in the ceiling panels of Britt's bedroom."

"No, I can't. But I can tell you where we first found the knife."

"Where?"

"Jeanette and I had watched your Piltdown Man movie in the theater room. After the movie, we went to the library to talk. We noticed the same lion figure in the movie was on the wall in the library. I thought I would turn it to see if anything happened like it did in the movie. Sure enough, when I turned it, the bookcase opened up and we found the hidden passageway. Needless to say, we were curious to see where it went, so we followed it all the way over to Britt's place."

"What about the knife?"

"When we came back, Jeanette and I found it wrapped in bloody rags hidden behind the stuffed bear in the passageway. I didn't want to disturb it because I knew it was evidence, so we left it there."

"I thought they found it in Britt's bedroom?" Phillip asked.

Jeanette turned to Phillip, "They did. We were going to tell the police but then I got a call from someone who sounded a lot like Moon Murchie telling me he had information about Britt's murder. He told us to meet him up at the cave."

"So who put the knife up in the ceiling tiles above Britt's bed?" Uncle Phil asked.

Stephen spoke up, "It had to be the killer trying to frame me."

Phillip rose from his chair. "I need to see where you found the knife, Stephen."

Chapter 43

Stephen and Jeanette followed Phillip up the staircase. When they got to the library, Phillip turned the lion head and the bookcase swung open. He entered the dark opening and turned on the light switch. They all entered the passageway.

"When I designed the manor, I tried to duplicate the house in the movie as much as possible. As you know, in the movie, the secret passageway goes to the Mad Doctor's hidden laboratory. Well, I didn't need a laboratory, but I thought it would be fun to have it go over to Britt's house. I never told her I had built this. The first time I used it, I scared her senseless. Britt was quietly reading a book, when suddenly the bookcase in her living room swung open and I stepped out. I thought it was quite a joke, but unfortunately, she didn't see the humor in it." As he spoke, Phillip ducked under the big model airplane hanging from the low ceiling.

Stephen stopped to look at the plane. "That looks like the plane the army used to attack the Piltdown Man in your movie."

"Yes it is. It's a model of a Curtiss Helldiver Naval training plane. You have a very good eye for detail, Stephen. It was also the same type of plane that shot down King Kong. That's where I got the idea."

Stephen took a step closer and touched the wing. "It's quite a model."

"The wingspan is over six feet wide and it's heavier than it looks. It's all metal. I keep it safe up here because I'll probably use it in a movie again sometime."

Stephen left the airplane and hurried to catch up to Jeanette and Phillip as they approached a turn in the corridor.

"This is where I screamed last time," Jeanette said to Phillip. "I didn't know you stored the big bear up here."

"I had to put it somewhere. Britt wanted me to get rid of it. I told her I may need to use it again as a prop so we agreed to keep it up here."

"Well, it really gave me a start when we were walking down the corridor last time," Jeanette said with a laugh.

Through the dim light, they spotted the huge stuffed bear halfway down the corridor, pushed against the wall. As they approached, the bear suddenly pivoted and moved towards them.

Jeanette muffled a scream as Phillip stopped and motioned for them to be quiet. Phillip watched as a shadowy figure struggled to lift something from inside of the bear's cavity.

A man emerged from behind the bear, stuffing clothes into a canvas bag.

Phillip stepped forward, "Bobby, what are you doing here?"

The guard looked up with a startled look on his face.

"Oh, Phillip…I'm, uh…I'm just cleaning up some trash I found."

"What sort of trash?" Phillip asked, as he reached for the bag.

Bobby swung the bag behind him and pulled a small revolver out of his waistband.

"Hold it, Phillip. Don't move."

Bobby's voice was suddenly different. It was a voice in command. Stephen had never heard Bobby speak to Phillip like that before.

Undaunted by the gun, Phillip moved closer to Bobby. The guard looked startled and let go of the bag. The bag opened as it hit the floor and a bloody shirt fell out.

"Stay back, Phillip, I'm warning you," Bobbie said.

"Bobby, what's going on here?" Phillip demanded.

"Just picking up some evidence," Bobby replied, as he shot a glare at Stephen.

"Evidence?" Phillip asked. "If this is evidence, we'll need it to help clear Stephen."

Phillip reached out to take the bag.

Bobby leveled the gun at Phillip. "You got a point there. Finding my bloody clothes would probably go a long way to clearing that nephew of yours, but it wouldn't do much for me."

Phillip looked surprised. "You? What do you have to do with any of this?" he asked.

"There's a lot you don't know, Phillip. Britt and I had plans. She showed me this passageway so I could come and see her whenever I wanted to."

"That's a lie!" Phillip shouted.

"No, I'm afraid it isn't. We were moving to Hollywood and she was going to get me some work."

Bobby turned to Stephen. "Britt and I had a great thing going until your nephew here showed up. Then, all of a sudden, our plans changed. I wasn't good enough anymore. Hollywood was out. Britt heard that Stephen's old man wrote Broadway plays. Now she wanted to be on Broadway. Britt thought I was just going to sit back and take being tossed aside like some washed up piece of crap."

Phillip interrupted, "Bobby, can't you see. Britt was just using you. Then, when Stephen arrived, she started using him, too. He had nothing to do with any of this."

"He should have gone back home when I pushed him over the log slide."

Stephen exclaimed, "That was you?"

Bobby continued, "It doesn't matter. She's history and I'm not taking the fall. That planted knife took any heat off me. Once I get rid of these bloody clothes, I'm in the clear."

"I don't think it's as easy as that, Bobby," Phillip said. He paused, watching Bobby's reaction. "So, now that we all know what happened, just give me the gun and this nightmare can all be over." Phillip held out his hand.

Bobby hesitated, looked down for a moment and then looked at Phillip.

"I don't think so." Bobby motioned to Stephen. "Untie that airplane prop behind you and toss me the ropes. Don't try anything funny, or I'll shoot your uncle and Jeanette, too."

Stephen reached up to the low ceiling and untied the ropes holding the airplane. He coiled the ropes into a tight ball and took a step towards Bobby. Bobby glanced over at Jeanette. Stephen reached back and threw the coiled ropes directly at Bobby's face.

Bobby fell backwards and a shot rang out from the revolver. A brilliant flash illuminated the dark corridor and Phillip clutched his shoulder. Jeanette screamed and rushed over to him. Jeanette could see a small trickle of blood begin to ooze through Phillip's fingers.

Bobby struggled to his feet and pushed Jeanette away from Phillip. He shoved the gun into Phillip's back and reached down to get the ropes Stephen had thrown at him.

"Tie up your nephew."

Phillip didn't move. Bobby aimed the gun near Phillip's head and squeezed off a round. Phillip ducked as he heard the bullet zip just past his head.

"Get moving," Bobby motioned with the gun.

Phillip walked over to Stephen. Stephen moved his hands behind his back. Paulie's words echoed in Stephen's head as Phillip started to tie him up. Stephen pushed the palms of his hands out slightly as Phillip wound the cord around his wrists. Phillip turned and faced Bobby when he was finished.

"Stephen, sit down and don't move." Bobby motioned with his gun, "Phillip, tie up Jeanette".

Bobby watched as Phillip was tying up Jeanette.

"I'm sorry, Phillip. But this is the way it has to be. When the cops find a double murder and suicide, the heat will be off me. I'll just go to Hollywood and make it on my own. To hell with Britt."

As Bobby talked, Stephen pushed his hands tightly together and felt the rope loosen. He looped his little finger around a coil and strained to pull it down. Slowly the loop inched free. He shook his hands and the cord fell from one hand. His hands were free.

Bobby stepped forward and pointed the gun to the side of Phillip's head. Stephen frantically searched the floor behind his back with his fingers. He grabbed on to something that was round and hard. It felt like some kind of wooden ball. With a flick of his wrist, he tossed the object down the corridor, trying hard not to move his arms or shoulders. The object rolled down the corridor and banged into a metal sign, knocking it over with a crash.

Bobby spun around and pointed the gun in the direction of the noise. Stephen bolted to his feet and slammed low into Bobby's knees, knocking him to the floor. The impact threw Bobby onto his back. Bobby squeezed off two rounds. Stephen grabbed for the revolver, trying to wrestle the gun away. Bobby hit Stephen in the face. Stephen grabbed Bobby's wrist with both hands. He pounded the revolver against the concrete floor.

Bobby let go of the gun, grabbing Stephen in a head lock and wrestling with him to the ground. They rolled into boxes, knocking movie props down around them. Bobby struggled to his feet, pulling Stephen up by his shirt. He punched Stephen in the stomach. Stephen stumbled backwards trying to catch his balance. Bobby reached down, tossing boxes aside as he searched for the gun.

Stephen saw a metallic glint as a box went sailing into the air. Bobby bent down to grab the gun. Stephen had rolled over next to the model airplane. He reached for the plane. It was heavy, much heavier than it looked. He raised the plane over his head and threw it at Bobby as hard as he could.

As Bobby rose with the gun, he saw something big sailing towards him. He tried to duck as the sharp wing of the airplane clipped his throat. Bobby tried to scream as he crumpled to the floor. He dropped the gun and frantically grabbed his throat with both hands as he gasped for breath.

Stephen rushed over, picked up the gun, and held it on Bobby as he untied Jeanette's hands. He handed the gun to Jeanette. "Make sure he doesn't try anything while I tie him up."

Bobby lay on his back as a pool of blood formed under his head. Stephen rolled him over and used the rope that had bound Jeanette to tie Bobby's hands. He double checked to make sure the binding was tight. Stephen ran over to his uncle.

"How's your shoulder?"

"It's not bad, the bullet just grazed me."

Stephen walked over to Jeanette and took back the gun.

"I'll stay here and cover Bobby. Jeanette, go call the police and an ambulance."

Phillip said, "I'll stay here with you, Stephen."

Chapter 44

It was three days later and Stella Moorhouse was sitting in the trophy room scrutinizing the group. Scott was sitting in a leather chair. King was lying on a rug at his feet. Stephen and Jeanette were sitting in the love seat, holding hands. Phillip was in his overstuffed chair next to the roaring fire. Joe walked in with his arm in a sling, eating a sandwich Cora had just slipped him.

Stella surveyed the crowd and then turned to Joe. "Before we begin, I want to ask Joe how is he doing?"

"I'm just fine, Mrs. Moorehouse. The doctor said I'll only have to wear this sling for a few more weeks."

"That's wonderful." She looked relieved. "Well, I think you have all changed my mind after all. Once Phillip decided to tell me what was really going on, I came out as soon as possible with the intention of bringing Stephen back to New York immediately."

"And what did I tell you, Stella?" Phillip asked with a smile.

"You said that everything was fine and that Stephen had made some wonderful friends. You told me the worst was over and he should be allowed to stay for the rest of the summer, as planned."

"And?" Stephen asked.

"After all the terrible things that had happened, I couldn't image allowing you to stay. But I must say, after spending the day with all of you, I think it would be best for Stephen to remain here and have the summer we all envisioned he would have."

A cheer went up from the crowd.

"But..," Stella interjected. "I have another plan."

A hush immediately filled the room.

"As you know, my husband Martin can not be with us today because he, very wisely, decided to seek treatment for his problem. I would very much like him to have the opportunity to meet all of you. It would be so wonderful if you could share your stories with Martin of how you all helped Stephen in his times of need. So, with that in mind, when Stephen returns to go to art school, I would love to have you all come for a visit and stay with us in New York City. I'll make all the arrangements and will pay for everyone's trip."

The room went wild. King stood up and started barking.

"Joe, did you ever think wearing that bear skin rug would wind up getting you a trip to New York City?" Scott asked.

"Since I've never even been across the Mackinac bridge to Lower Michigan, I'd have to say that would be a no!" Joe laughed.

"And, Jeanette," Stella said.

Jeanette turned from Scott and Joe.

"Yes?"

"I think you may have to come a few days early, since after talking to Stephen, it looks like the Moorhouse family will be seeing quite a bit more of you in the future."

Jeanette turned a pretty shade of pink, poked Stephen in the arm and said, "Oh, Stephen!"

21787047R00109

Made in the USA
Charleston, SC
30 August 2013